F...
NANC...

THE CASE: Investigate the fiery destruction of a priceless portrait of Napoleon.

CONTACT: Preston Talbot, *president of Victory Airlines and owner of the Victory Hotel, where the mysterious fire erupted in a locked vault.*

SUSPECTS: Peter Wellington—*an eccentric antiques dealer. He's been fingered by Brent Kincaid, the owner of the portrait, as the prime suspect.*

Sheik Abdullah—*the handsome billionaire who owned the portrait before Brent Kincaid won it from him.*

Nicole Ronsarde—*the French professor and book collector who planned to buy a valuable Napoleonic manuscript before a former student maliciously outbid her.*

Chad Bannister—*the hunk who's been asking a lot of questions about the portrait on his own time.*

COMPLICATIONS: Two other Napoleonic treasures have gone up in smoke, and Nancy's trying to discover the connection. Meanwhile, Elaine Ellsworth, an insurance investigator, is keeping a careful eye on Nancy.

Books in The Nancy Drew Files® Series

Available from ARCHWAY Paperbacks

THE NANCY DREW FILES™ CASE · 26

PLAYING WITH FIRE

Carolyn Keene

AN ARCHWAY PAPERBACK
Published by POCKET BOOKS
New York   London   Toronto   Sydney   Tokyo   Singapore

AN ARCHWAY PAPERBACK *Original*

An Archway Paperback published by
POCKET BOOKS, a division of Simon & Schuster Inc.
1230 Avenue of the Americas, New York, NY 10020

Copyright © 1988 by Simon & Schuster Inc.
Cover art copyright © 1988 Jim Mathewuse
Produced by Mega-Books of New York, Inc.

ISBN: 0-671-70356-0

First Archway Paperback printing August 1988

10 9 8 7 6 5 4 3

Printed in the U.S.A.

IL 7+

PLAYING WITH FIRE

Chapter

One

W OW!" GEORGE FAYNE exclaimed as she peered out the window of the Victory Airlines jumbo jet. "What an incredible city! It's enormous!"

Nancy Drew leaned in from her aisle seat to look over her friend's shoulder for a glimpse of Los Angeles. "It *is* big," she agreed. "And look—you can see the ocean!"

The huge 747 jet had just crossed the rugged San Gabriel Mountains and was beginning its long, smooth glide toward Los Angeles International Airport. Below them the city stretched from the mountains to the coast, an endless carpet of houses, office buildings, and shopping malls carved into strange geometric shapes by

1

the curving freeways. On the horizon lay the calm Pacific, blue and gleaming.

George turned away from the window and ran her fingers through her dark, tousled hair. "When do you suppose Bess is coming back from the cockpit?" she asked as the seat-belt sign over their heads blinked on.

Grinning, Nancy fastened her belt. "Probably in a minute or two," she said. "I doubt Mark will let her land this monster."

Bess Marvin, George's pretty blond cousin, had been riding in the aisle seat right across from Nancy and George. But right after they'd boarded the plane, she learned from the flight attendant that the copilot was an old friend, Mark Thompson. After takeoff she'd run a comb through her hair and checked her eye makeup before disappearing in the direction of the cockpit to renew her friendship.

Bess had met Mark when she was working undercover as a flight attendant on a case Nancy solved for the president of Victory Airlines, Preston Talbot. It was that case—*Wings of Fear*—that was responsible for their being on the jumbo jet now.

"You still haven't told us exactly why Mr. Talbot is giving us an all-expense-paid trip to Los Angeles," George reminded Nancy, stretching her arms above her head. "I'm not knocking it—a chance to spend some time in the California sun—but I'm still curious to know why he needs us."

"I know you are," Nancy said. "But you did sleep the whole flight, and we might as well wait to talk about it until Bess gets back. Okay?"

George nodded and leaned back and yawned. "Well, whatever Mr. Talbot has in mind for us, I have to admit that going first class is great. These seats are big enough for two people to share."

Nancy smiled without answering. She was thinking that if she could share her seat with anyone, it would be her boyfriend, Ned Nickerson. Nancy wished Ned could have come with them on this new case, but he had a special project due at his school, Emerson College.

Still, he had taken time off to drive Nancy and her friends to Chicago's O'Hare Airport for their 8 A.M. Saturday flight. Ned had held Nancy back as the other two climbed out of the car. He had given her a warm hug and a lingering last-minute kiss. She could still feel the touch of his lips on hers, and his warm arms . . .

"I'm back!" Bess was bubbling, sliding into her seat and fastening her belt. She leaned across the aisle toward Nancy. "You should *see* all the controls Mark has to handle to make this thing fly." Her eyes sparkled. "I just love to watch him. I don't see how he remembers it all."

3

"He *does* get some help from the pilot and the flight engineer, doesn't he?" George asked dryly.

Nancy pushed her tote bag under the seat. "And from the autopilot and the on-board computer?"

Bess dismissed their teasing with a careless wave of her hand. "Anyway, he said he'd call me at the hotel later. I can't wait."

"Now that Bess is back," George said, turning to Nancy, "you'd better brief us on this case." The plane was banking in a wide turn, heading for its final descent onto the airport runway a few miles ahead.

Nancy nodded, her face serious. "I told you that Mr. Talbot called me yesterday." Bess and George nodded. "It seems that his airline owns the Victory Hotel in Los Angeles. There was a suspicious fire at the hotel on Thursday— probably arson—and he's worried.

"The fire was in the hotel vault," Nancy went on, "and the cash receipts for the entire week were burned. But Mr. Talbot thinks the target was an antique miniature portrait of Napoleon. One of his guests had asked to have it put in the vault for safekeeping. The owner had apparently received an extortion note, and thought it would be safer in the hotel vault than at his bank." Nancy paused. "There's no way to be sure what the real target was, though. Or even if it was arson. Everything in the vault was a total

4

loss, and the fire destroyed any clues to how it got started."

Bess looked puzzled. "Sounds like arson. But how could anyone start a fire in a *locked* vault and get out?"

"That's what we've got to find out. The hotel's insurance company wants the fire investigated, but Mr. Talbot doesn't want the police to be involved—at least for the time being. He's worried that news of the fire might leak out. Victory Hotel is hosting some big society gala next week, and he wants to make sure it's a success. He's afraid that any bad publicity will keep people away."

"Is there a chance that a hotel employee might be involved?" George asked.

"There's a good chance," Nancy replied. "Anyway, I think we should start by interviewing the employees. Mr. Talbot is meeting us at the airport, and we'll be staying at the hotel. That'll keep us close to any possible suspects."

The landing wheels of the jet hit the runway with a jolt, jarring Nancy in her seat. "Mr. Talbot's also promised to lend us a car," she added.

Bess smiled happily. "First class all the way," she said with a sigh. "I love it." She glanced at Nancy and George. "Listen, would you guys mind if I took tonight off? I mean, I know we're here to work, but I have the feeling that Mark is going to ask me to dinner when he calls, and—"

Nancy grinned. "And you just can't turn him down. Right?"

Bess blushed. "Do you mind?" she asked anxiously.

Nancy waved her hand. "No, go ahead," she said. "George and I can handle tonight. But we will all work today, and by tomorrow we should be really busy."

"Nancy Drew!" Mr. Talbot strode out of the crowd in the airport corridor, his hand stretched out to her. "I'm glad you're here. Did you have a pleasant flight?"

Mr. Talbot was a tall, well-dressed man with gray hair. He was smiling, but the smile didn't quite disguise the tension in his face. Obviously the problem at the hotel was causing him deep concern. He had even moved temporarily to Los Angeles.

"It was a wonderful flight," Nancy said. "You certainly know how to please your passengers." She turned to George. "Mr. Talbot, I'd like you to meet my friend George Fayne. And you remember Bess Marvin, of course."

"Of course," Mr. Talbot said cordially. "I'm glad that both of you could come along. This isn't going to be an easy case, I'm afraid. It—" He broke off and turned back to glance at someone standing a couple of feet behind him. "Oh, yes. I'd like you to meet Brent Kincaid. He's the owner of the portrait that was destroyed in the hotel vault. His father is an old friend of mine, and they own Kincaid Studios here in L.A. Brent is staying at the hotel while renovations are being done on his house."

Brent Kincaid stepped forward. He was a tall, deeply tanned young man with smooth dark hair and intense brown eyes. He smiled admiringly at Nancy as he shook her hand.

"Mr. Talbot has told me about you," he said. "According to him, you're a top detective with a pretty impressive record. I'm fascinated by mysteries. We film a lot of them, and I'm always interested in detectives and crime. I must say, though," he added appraisingly, "that I wouldn't have guessed you're a detective. You're much too pretty."

Nancy swung her woven straw tote bag over one shoulder and slid her brown leather purse over the other. "Thanks," she said briefly. She was used to people's surprise when they learned that she was a detective, but she wasn't accustomed to the outright flattery she'd heard in Brent Kincaid's voice. "It's too bad about the portrait. But I hope we can wrap the case up in a hurry."

"I hope so, too, Nancy," Mr. Talbot said as he started to lead the way down the crowded corridor toward the baggage-claim area. "This whole thing could be very embarrassing for the hotel. The more quickly it's solved, the better."

Suddenly a group of noisy, flashily dressed

teenage girls brushed past them. One had bright green hair, another was dressed in a skintight black leotard and a red metallic tunic, and a third was wearing a micro-mini purple skirt and knee-high purple boots. She had a purple tattoo just above her right knee.

George turned to stare. "Is *that* what they're wearing in L.A. these days?" she asked. She looked down at her peg pants, black ankle boots, and oversize blue cotton sweater. "I feel kind of underdressed."

Brent Kincaid laughed. "Remember," he said, "Hollywood is just minutes from here. This is a crazy town. You're likely to see anything—and anything is likely to happen." As they moved around a corner, he gestured toward a luggage carousel that was just beginning to turn. "Your bags should be out in a minute," he said. "Will you excuse me? I have to make a phone call."

"I'll go get a skycap," Mr. Talbot said. "Then we can go right to the hotel."

"Fine," Nancy replied. She turned toward the carousel as Mr. Talbot and Brent Kincaid walked away. "I'm glad we're traveling light," she said, with a teasing grin at Bess. Bess had brought only two suitcases this time, both of them stuffed to bursting.

But Bess wasn't listening. "I think I smell something—like smoke," she said.

George frowned at her. "Don't say things like

that, Bess," she cautioned. "You could start a real panic in this crowd."

"But it's true," Bess insisted. "I mean, I really *do* smell—" She grabbed Nancy's arm. "Nancy!" she shrieked. "It's your tote bag! I think you're on fire!"

Chapter

Two

Nancy slipped the smoking tote bag off her shoulder. Holding it at arm's length, she shoved her way through the crowd and out the automatic door. Then she flung it into the street—right in front of a parked taxi.

There was a loud explosion and a brilliant flash of light. Nancy watched in horror as her bag disappeared in a cloud of white smoke and scattered debris.

"A bomb!" Bess exclaimed from right behind Nancy. She and George had just caught up. "Somebody dropped a bomb into your bag!"

"Who threw that bag into the street?" An airport security officer rushed toward them, his gun drawn.

"I did," Nancy explained breathlessly. Her

heart was still beating double time from the shock of the near miss. "It was on fire—"

"You're under arrest," the guard snapped. "Put your hands on your head."

"You're making a mistake, officer!" George protested. "Somebody *planted* that bomb in Nancy's bag."

"You two with her?" the guard asked George and Bess. George nodded.

"Hands on your heads too," the guard growled. He pointed at Nancy. "You—got any identification?"

Nancy slowly took her hands down and opened her purse to pull out her driver's license.

"We're here as the guests of Mr. Talbot," Bess wailed. "You know, the president of Victory Airlines."

The guard grinned. "Yeah, and *I'm* here as the guest of the president of the United States," he said.

Mr. Talbot elbowed his way through the crowd. "What's going on here?" he demanded. Nancy had barely started explaining when Mr. Talbot pulled out his wallet and showed his identification to the guard. "I'll vouch for them," he said.

The guard stared openmouthed at Mr. Talbot. Nancy almost expected him to salute. Quickly he holstered his gun. "Yes, sir," he said meekly.

Mr. Talbot turned to Nancy. "Now, Nancy, start over. What happened?"

"It looks as though somebody slipped something into my tote bag," Nancy said. "Something designed to fry anything near it." She stepped into the street and began to poke at the charred remains of her bag.

George and Bess followed her.

"Find anything?" George asked.

Nancy shook her head ruefully. "There's not much left—and not a sign of whatever triggered the explosion." She frowned. "It's weird. There ought to be something left of the device that caused it. It must have been super-sophisticated to have completely disappeared."

"I guess anybody could have stuck anything in your bag," Bess said. "But it was so crowded that there's no hope of finding out *who.*"

Nancy nodded. "You're right," she said. "And there's no way of finding out whether this bomb was meant for *us* or not. Either it has some connection to this case, or else it's just the work of some sickie."

George shivered. "Welcome to L.A.," she muttered.

"So there you are! I've been looking all over for you. I made my call," Brent Kincaid announced as the automatic doors opened and he walked through them. "Are we ready to— What's going on?" He stopped short, staring at Nancy digging at the remains of her bag.

"Well—" Bess started to answer him but was interrupted by the guard, who appeared to be coming out of a fog.

"I do have to ask you to come to the office," the officer said, with a quick glance at Mr. Talbot. "I'll need to fill out a report on this incident."

Mr. Talbot nodded. "Of course. We might as well get this over with," he told Nancy.

It took only a few minutes to answer the guard's questions. When he'd finished filling out the report form, he carefully set his pencil back in a jar. "Those *are* the facts," he said. "But I'd like to know what *really* happened."

Nancy stood up slowly, saying, "You're not the only one."

Mr. Talbot got up then, too. "If there are any further questions," he said, "you can reach Miss Drew at the Victory Hotel."

"Whew," George said, flopping down onto a velvety sofa in the Victory Hotel's executive suite. "I'm sure glad *that's* over." She grinned at Nancy. "Any more bombs up your sleeve, Nancy?"

"Don't even mention bombs," Bess said with a shudder. She glanced up from the desk where she was leafing through a newspaper and looked admiringly at the mauve and blue upholstered sofa and chairs, the mirrored wall, the vases of fresh flowers on every polished dark wood table.

13

"What a super suite! Talk about plush! Mr. Talbot certainly knows how to treat his guests."

"Now we'll just have to do everything we can to deserve it," Nancy said as she walked into one of the bedrooms. She unzipped her suitcase and began to unpack the clothes she had brought—one favorite dressy outfit for dinner, a couple of casual skirts, and jeans for daytime. "He looks as though he's lost a lot of sleep over all this," she called into the living room. "I hope we can figure out what happened in a hurry."

"What's our plan?" George asked, following Nancy into the bedroom.

"I'm interviewing the chief of hotel security at eleven, and Brent Kincaid asked me to have lunch with him at noon." She glanced over at George. "It's possible *he's* involved. His painting was bound to have been insured, and he could make big bucks from the fire."

"Maybe so," George said. "What do you want Bess and me to do?"

"Talk to the clerk who checks items into the vault. Maybe he'll remember something that—" Nancy broke off as Bess came into the room with the newspaper in her hand.

"Nancy!" Bess said excitedly. "Somebody in this town has a grudge against Napoleon! Look!" She pointed to a headline on the society page. It read, "Flaming *Napoleon* Still Unsolved."

Nancy took the paper and sat down beside

George. "'Wealthy book collector Amanda Hyde-Porter,'" she read aloud, "'is still mourning the loss of her valuable manuscript, *Napoleon and Josephine*. The original handwritten draft of François LaMotte's famous play was mysteriously burned last week while it was under close security in her Bel Air mansion. Police confess they have no clues in the baffling case.'"

"Wow!" George said breathily. "Another torching!"

"Yeah," Nancy said grimly. "It looks as if our arsonist has a Napoleon fixation, doesn't it? I have the feeling that this is going to be a *very* interesting case!"

It was noon. Nancy stepped inside the lavishly decorated hotel dining room and looked around. Brent Kincaid was sitting alone at a corner table. As she walked up to him, he stood quickly and pulled out her chair with a polite flourish.

"Thank you, Mr. Kincaid," she said.

"Please—call me Brent," he said.

Nancy smiled. "Thank you, Brent." She picked up her menu and studied it for a minute. "Everything looks great. What do you recommend?"

"Well, you *are* in California. Why don't you try something a little different? Perhaps the warm duck salad with raspberry vinegar and

15

baby vegetables? I'm having the squid-ink pasta myself."

Nancy winced inwardly. "The salad sounds fine."

After the waitress had taken their orders, Brent put his elbows on the table and leaned in toward Nancy. "Well, Mademoiselle Detective, have you solved our mystery yet?" he asked.

"Not yet," Nancy admitted. She wasn't going to admit it to Brent, but her forty-five-minute interview with the hotel security chief had yielded nothing beyond what she already knew. The cash receipts had been in the safe all week, but Brent hadn't put the Napoleon miniature in the vault until Thursday night, just before eight. The alarm had gone off at 3 A.M. Friday. The guard had opened the vault to find a smoldering pile of ashes. There were absolutely no physical clues to the cause of the fire, and the security chief had told Nancy that the arson investigators from the insurance company were utterly baffled. They'd spent hours looking for some trace of an incendiary device, but they'd found nothing.

"Well, perhaps I can help you a bit," Brent said. "As you know, I'm staying in the hotel while my house is being redecorated. On Wednesday night I returned to my suite and found an extortion note under my door. It demanded a million dollars in twenty-four hours—or the Napoleon would be destroyed."

He broke off to smile at the waitress as she brought them their cold watercress and zucchini soup. "I've given the note to the insurance investigators, of course."

"Was there anything distinctive about the note?" Nancy asked. "Handwriting, paper, anything like that?"

Brent picked up his spoon. "The letters had been hand-stenciled, so the handwriting couldn't be traced. But the paper *was* distinctive, I guess—gray with a thin red border." He flashed Nancy a smile. "By the way, I hope you're not considering *me* a suspect. If you are, I can tell you that you're wrong."

Nancy looked at him. "Why?" she asked quietly. "Why *aren't* you a suspect?"

"Because the painting wasn't insured," Brent replied calmly, dipping his spoon into his soup.

Nancy frowned. "But you just said that you gave the note to the insurance investigators—"

"The *hotel's* insurance investigators," Brent corrected her. "I'd just acquired the miniature a few days earlier, and I hadn't insured it yet. I've already told Mr. Talbot that if the hotel's insurance pays up, I'll donate the money to charity. There's no way the miniature can be replaced, and I'm not interested in making money out of it. That would give me the creeps."

"Do you know anybody who might have a motive to destroy your painting?" Nancy asked.

Brent shrugged. "Not really. I know somebody who's *crazy* enough to do it," he said. "His name's Peter Wellington. He owns an antique shop out in Venice. He says his antiques are for sale, but I suspect that he's more of a collector than a dealer. Anyway, he was after me for days to let him buy the painting. I kept saying no, but he wouldn't give up. He's a real nut. Maybe he figured that if he couldn't have it, nobody—"

He broke off abruptly and shook his head. "But I'm probably wrong," he said. "At this point I'm willing to suspect anyone. I'm sure Wellington's harmless."

"I wonder," Nancy said thoughtfully, "whether he might be interested in manuscripts."

Brent's head snapped up. "Manuscripts?"

Nancy handed Brent the newspaper clipping Bess had shown her. "It's possible that the two crimes are connected," she said.

Brent studied the clipping and handed it back. "It does look as if our arsonist might have had two targets," he agreed. "Would you like to meet Amanda, by the way? I could arrange an introduction."

"You know her?" Nancy asked.

"We took classes together at UCLA several years ago. We bump into each other occasionally."

"Yes, I *would* like to talk to Amanda," Nancy said. "Maybe she could give us a lead on—"

"Mr. Brent Kincaid?" someone interrupted.

18

Nancy looked up. A steely-eyed woman dressed in a tailored business suit was standing beside their table. Her ash blond hair was pulled back into a bun, and she carried a slim leather briefcase. As Brent Kincaid stood up, she held out her hand and said crisply, "I'm Elaine Ellsworth, with Pacific Insurance. I'm helping to investigate the fire. I believe you spoke with my colleague, Al Lawson."

"Of course," Brent said, shaking her hand. "This is Nancy Drew. She's a pri—"

"I work for Preston Talbot," Nancy interrupted quickly.

Ms. Ellsworth acknowledged Nancy with a cool nod. Then she turned back to Brent. "Could we meet in Mr. Talbot's office at three this afternoon?" she asked. "I have some questions for you."

"Sure," Brent said. "You don't want to talk right now?"

Ms. Ellsworth shook her head. "I'd prefer to meet privately, if you don't mind." Her eyes flicked briefly at Nancy. "At three, then," she said, and she walked briskly away.

"Well," Brent said after Ms. Ellsworth had gone, "looks as though you're going to have some help with your case."

Nancy only nodded. She wasn't sure that Elaine Ellsworth was the kind of help she needed.

* * *

"So you drew a blank when you talked to the hotel clerk," Nancy said, pulling Mr. Talbot's white Lincoln up to the curb in front of Amanda Hyde-Porter's house.

George nodded. "He couldn't tell us a thing," she said. "He inspected the painting when he checked it into the vault, but he didn't notice anything out of the ordinary." She shook her head with a puzzled look. "I just don't get it. If the arsonist had used an incendiary device, wouldn't it have left some kind of residue?"

Bess shivered. "Maybe it's something supernatural. I'm reading this novel where a little girl can start fires just by *thinking* about—"

Nancy gave her a look. "Natural or supernatural," she said, "we're left with nothing to go on. I talked to Mr. Talbot. He confirmed the fact that Brent's portrait wasn't insured and that Brent promised to donate anything he gets from the insurance company to charity. So it looks as though we can take Brent off our list of suspects." She glanced at her watch. "We'd better stop sitting here and get out of the car. Amanda Hyde-Porter is expecting us."

"So this is how people live in Bel Air," Bess said a little enviously. The whole street was lined with huge, expensive houses securely nestled behind lush green hedges.

The Hyde-Porter house was a white brick mansion. Marble steps led up to its dark mahogany front door with a gleaming brass lion's-head knocker. "I wonder," George mused as they walked up the three steps, "how many movie stars live in this block."

"Movie stars?" Bess squealed. "Do you really think——"

"Shh," Nancy cautioned. "I hear someone coming."

The front door opened, and a young woman stood looking at them. Her shining dark hair was pulled dramatically over one ear. She was wearing a white silk tunic over white silk pants and Egyptian thong sandals. She made Nancy feel very young and unsophisticated.

"Amanda?" Nancy asked. The woman nodded. "I'm Nancy Drew," Nancy said. "And these are my friends, Bess Marvin and George Fayne. Brent Kincaid suggested that we talk with you about the Napoleon manuscript."

"I was expecting you," Amanda said. "Come in." They stepped onto the black- and white-checkered marble floor of the foyer. Amanda led them into an enormous library, lined floor to ceiling with books.

Nancy looked around. She had never seen so many books in a private home—and many of them looked valuable, if she could judge by their leather and gilt bindings. "This is quite a collection," she said.

"My father's," Amanda said shortly. "I inherited it. Mostly. I *have* bought one or two volumes, and I've sold one or two pieces. I was preparing to sell the Napoleon manuscript, which I had bought. In fact, I even had a buyer who had made a fabulous offer. Unfortunately, it was a lot more than the insurance company is willing to pay." She gestured toward some leather chairs, and the girls all sat. "I'm not sure why Brent thought we should talk," she said. "The insurance company is handling the investigation, and I don't really have anything to—"

"He suggested it," Nancy said, "because he thought there might be a connection between your loss and his."

Amanda raised her carefully shaped eyebrows. *"His* loss? I don't understand."

Nancy told her briefly about the burning of the Napoleon miniature and the extortion note Brent had received. "Are any of the details of Brent's case similar to yours?" she finished.

"Well, there is one similarity," Amanda said, tapping her manicured nails on the arm of her chair. "I also got an extortion note on gray notepaper with a red border. It said pretty much the same thing—that I had twenty-four hours to come up with the money, or else I'd lose the manuscript."

"You decided not to pay up?" George asked.

Amanda's dark eyes were cool, her face calm. "I don't like extortion," she said. "I called the police immediately. They put a guard on the room where the manuscript was kept. But the guard was totally useless. The next morning, I discovered—"

There was a squeal of tires just then in the drive outside, followed by the sound of the front door banging open. "Amanda!" a woman's voice cried hysterically. "Amanda, where are you?"

"I'm in the library, Diana," Amanda called.

They heard feet racing through the hall, and then a redheaded young woman burst in through the doorway. She was dressed in green silk pants and a blue shirt, with heavy gold chains around her neck and gold bracelets clanking on both wrists. With a theatrical gesture, she flung her arms into the air.

"Oh, Amanda!" she wailed tragically. "They're going to destroy Josephine's dress! You have to help me stop them!"

Amanda stood up and took the young woman by the shoulders. "Calm down, Diana," she said in a firm voice, "and tell me what happened."

"What happened?" Diana said shrilly, collapsing dramatically onto a sofa. "If I don't come up with a million dollars by tomorrow night, the Empress's Flame will be destroyed!"

Chapter

Three

Bess LOOKED CONFUSED. "Flame?" she asked. "They're going to destroy a flame?"

"It's a dress," Amanda told her. "Diana owns a world-famous collection of old clothes. One piece is called the Empress's Flame. It's a valuable old dress—"

Diana sat up and began to dry her eyes. "It's a priceless *antique* dress," she said emphatically. "It was worn by the empress Josephine at her husband's coronation—"

"Napoleon's?" Nancy asked, interrupting. Three cases of extortion and arson involving Napoleonic relics—they *had* to be related.

Diana nodded. Tears brimmed in her eyes again. "Amanda, where am I going to get a million dollars by tomorrow night? I know what

24

happened to your manuscript and Brent's miniature. They'll get the dress and burn it—I know they will. And you know I don't have any—"

Amanda patted Diana's shoulder gently. "Now, stop worrying, Diana," she said, comforting her friend. "I'm sure we can stop them somehow. It's lucky you came when you did. This is Nancy Drew," she added, nodding toward Nancy. "She's a famous detective. Maybe she and her associates can help you."

"Oh, could you?" Diana exclaimed. She cast a wide-eyed, hopeful look at Nancy and the others. "If you could do something—anything —to save the Empress's Flame, I'd be so grateful."

"Do you happen to have the extortion note with you?" Nancy asked.

"I do," Diana said. She fished in the pocket of her pants and pulled out a crumpled piece of gray paper. She thrust it at Nancy. *"Keep* the awful thing," she said, her voice breaking dramatically. "I don't want to look at it again."

Nancy smoothed the note. " 'It'll cost you a million to keep the Flame,' " she read aloud. " 'You have until tomorrow night to find the money.' "

George looked at Amanda. "Is this the same paper your extortion note was written on?" she asked.

Amanda nodded. "I recognize the red border. My note also asked for a million dollars."

"But I don't *have* a million!" Diana cried, burying her face in her hands.

"But maybe you have another choice," Amanda interrupted. "Maybe Nancy could guard the Flame. That is, if you'd be willing, Nancy."

But Nancy thought of a better idea. "How about substituting a copy of the Flame?" she asked. "That way, the original would be safe while we used the copy to trap the arsonist."

"Great idea!" Amanda said enthusiastically. She turned to Diana. "I know a costumer for one of the studios who could easily make a copy of the Flame. She works incredibly fast, too. Do you have a photo of the dress? I think she could work from that."

Diana nodded eagerly. "I've got the perfect shot," she said.

"Wonderful," Nancy said. She looked at the note again. "I think the real dress is safe until tomorrow evening. But you'd better arrange for a police guard starting sometime tomorrow afternoon."

"A police guard?" Diana wailed. "But what about my *party?* Tomorrow I'm giving my biggest party of the year, and I can't have the police crawling all over my house. They'd *ruin* everything!"

"Well, in that case," Amanda asked reasonably, "would you be willing to guard the dress, Nancy?"

"Oh, please say you will, Nancy," Diana said plaintively.

Nancy thought quickly. Being on the scene would give her a much better chance to catch the extortionist. "I'll be happy to guard it," she said. "I think we should swap dresses and set up the guard in the afternoon. If the dress is ready, that is."

She turned to Amanda. "I asked Brent to suggest any possible suspects in the case. Can you think of anyone who might have a motive for these crimes?"

Amanda looked troubled. "There is one person, but—no, I guess she wouldn't be . . ." Her voice trailed off, and Nancy wondered if she was trying to protect someone. "Well, you might at least want to talk to her," Amanda said at last. "Her name's Professor Nicole Ronsarde, and I don't think there's anyone in the world who hates Napoleon as much as she does."

"Hates Napoleon?" Bess asked blankly. "Why would anybody hate somebody who's been dead for a couple hundred years? It doesn't sound rational."

Amanda shook her head sadly. "That's just the point. It *isn't* rational. Professor Ronsarde can trace her family back to the time of Napoleon. One of her ancestors was tortured by Napoleon. She's a real nut on the subject—she just hates him. I know all this because I was a student of hers once."

It sounded to Nancy as if Professor Ronsarde would be worth investigating. "Where can I find her?" Nancy asked.

"She lives on a houseboat at Marina del Rey," Amanda told her. "I can give you the dock number." She turned solicitously to Diana. "Are you feeling better now?"

"Oh, yes," Diana said cheerfully. "Now that I know the Flame will be safe, I can enjoy my party. Amanda, you have the *best* ideas."

"Why don't you give Nancy your address, Diana?" Amanda suggested. "She and her friends can be on their way while I call the costumer and help you with your plans for tomorrow."

Diana jotted down her address and handed it to Nancy. "I live in Beverly Hills. Come dressed for a party," she said to the three girls, smiling happily. "We'll have a fabulous time."

"What a flake," George muttered as they walked down the circular drive to Mr. Talbot's car. "That Diana's a character."

"Yes, but a *party*," Bess said, her eyes sparkling. "A real Beverly Hills party! I wonder what we should wear?"

"We're not going to be guests, Bess," Nancy reminded her. "Probably no one will even see us. But tonight you'll get a chance to party. Mark's taking you out, isn't he?"

"Uh-huh," Bess said, and she fell into a daydream, forgetting everything but Mark.

The next morning the girls drove south from Los Angeles to Venice, a colorful community of artists' shops and inviting-looking restaurants clustered picturesquely beside the ocean. As they walked along the famous Venice boardwalk, they constantly had to dodge skateboarders and rollerskaters.

"Everyone's on wheels here!" Bess said, giggling. It was her first real comment of the day. All she'd done till then was sigh and say what a great time she'd had with Mark. That was it—nothing else.

"Look, Nancy, isn't that what we're after?" George asked, pointing to a sign in a window.

Nancy glanced up. They were standing in front of a tiny shop. On its window, in ornate gold letters, was printed WELLINGTON'S ART AND ANTIQUES. The shade was pulled down, so the girls couldn't see inside. A sign on the door said, "Open at 11."

Nancy glanced at her watch. "It's ten-thirty," she said. "Let's have something to drink while we wait for Peter Wellington."

The girls headed across the street toward a small café with bright red sidewalk tables. They chose a table in the sunshine, ordered lemonade, and sat back to watch the parade of people on the boardwalk.

"Wow, look at that tan," Bess exclaimed as a guy walked into the café balancing a surfboard on his head. "And those muscles! What a hunk!"

"Watch it, Bess." George laughed. "You might forget Mark." She turned just then and saw a guy step off a skateboard and prop it up against a table while he ordered iced tea. His T-shirt was blazoned with the words "Skateboard Champion." "Champion, huh?" she muttered skeptically. "I'll bet I could show *him* a trick or two on that skateboard."

Nancy laughed and leaned back in her chair. George, a gifted athlete, could never resist a challenge. "Go to it, George," she teased.

Then she frowned. The door of Wellington's shop—the door that bore the "Closed" sign— had just opened. A handsome, dark-bearded young man stepped out, looked around furtively as if to be sure he wasn't being followed, and disappeared around the corner.

"I wonder who that is?" Nancy murmured. "Let's go over and check it out."

Bess paid the tab and joined Nancy and George across the street. Nancy tried the doorknob of the shop. It turned easily. The three girls slipped inside.

The shop was in deep shadow. Only a dim, dusty light filtered in around the front window shade. Nancy shivered, wrinkling her nose against the musty odor of old books. In the darkness she heard a clock ticking and the eerie tinkling of a small mechanical music box.

The walls of the tiny shop were covered with floor-to-ceiling shelves filled with dusty antiques: old-fashioned gold jewelry, leather-bound books, a pair of tarnished swords, a plumed soldier's helmet. Mysterious shapes loomed out at them from the shadows, and a gilt-framed portrait of Napoleon frowned solemnly down from high on a wall.

"This is like a museum," Bess whispered.

Nancy looked around. The shop *was* like a museum, and she'd have bet that nothing had been sold out of it for years. No wonder Brent had said that Wellington was more of a collector than a dealer. The man who had gathered all this stuff must be at least a little crazy, she thought. But was he crazy enough to want to destroy a painting he couldn't add to his collection? And what about Amanda's manuscript and the Empress's Flame?

Suddenly there was a muted clatter from the back of the shop. Nancy and her friends stiffened. A dusty velvet curtain covering the doorway to the back stirred for an instant as if touched by a sudden wind and then parted slightly. And in the next second Nancy found herself looking down the gaping muzzle of an antique musket!

Chapter
Four

WHAT ARE YOU girls doing in my shop?" a voice demanded crankily from behind the curtain. "Didn't you see the sign on the door?"

"But we saw someone come out," Nancy managed to say while staring at the musket. "And we thought you were open." The gun looked too old to do much damage, but she couldn't be sure. She swallowed. "Would you mind putting that gun down? It's making me nervous."

Still holding the musket, a man emerged from behind the green velvet curtain. He looked as if he were in his sixties, with wispy gray hair and a straggly Van Dyke beard. A red paisley shawl was draped over his stooped shoulders. He peered down at the gun cradled in his arm.

"Gun? Oh, yes. Pardon me, ladies. I was adjusting the flintlock, you see, and—" Suddenly he scowled at them. "You haven't answered my question. What do you want? Didn't you see the sign on the door?"

"We'd like some information," Nancy said. "My name is Nancy Drew. I'm a private detective, and I'm investigating a case of arson. Brent Kincaid's miniature portrait of Napoleon was burned on Friday. Do you know anything about it?"

Peter Wellington cackled scornfully. "What do I know? I know it was a case of just retribution, *that's* what I know. That painting was never meant to be owned by Kincaid. Why, he wouldn't know an antique from a piece of junk. And just look at the way he got his hands on it. Dishonest, that's what *I* say."

Nancy's ears pricked up. "Just how *did* Brent acquire the miniature?" she asked. "And how much did he pay for it?"

Wellington laughed sarcastically. "Why, young lady, it didn't cost him a penny. Brent Kincaid *won* that miniature—in a poker game."

"A poker game?" George repeated.

"Kincaid is L.A.'s biggest playboy gambler," Wellington said, emphasizing his words with a wave of the musket. "He won that miniature from Sheik Abdullah."

"Sheik *who?*" Nancy asked incredulously.

"Sheik Hassan Karim Abdullah," Wellington said. "Lives in the most expensive house in Malibu." He peered craftily at Nancy. "If I were trying to solve this case, I'd have a serious talk with Abdullah. Maybe the sheik didn't take kindly to losing his favorite portrait."

"And you?" Nancy asked quickly. "How did *you* feel when Kincaid refused to sell you the miniature?"

Wellington turned and put the gun in a rack on the wall. Beside Nancy, Bess breathed an audible sigh of relief. "You win some, you lose some," Wellington replied. "At my age, I'm philosophical about such things. But I do hate to see a fine piece like that destroyed. It was a shame about the fire."

Nancy frowned. What Wellington had said sounded reasonable enough, but he had avoided her eyes when he answered the question. Did he know more than he was telling her?

"I must say, the subject seems to be a popular one," Wellington went on. "The young man who was in here just before you also asked about Kincaid's miniature."

"A young man? Did he have a beard?" Nancy asked, remembering the guy she'd seen furtively leaving the shop.

Wellington nodded.

"Did you get his name?"

"Never thought to ask it. He wanted to know about other local collectors of Napoleonic rel-

34

ics. I gave him some names—Amanda Hyde-Porter, Diana Normandy—"

Nancy cleared her throat. "Diana Normandy? Doesn't she own the Empress's Flame?" she asked casually.

Wellington nodded. "A real jewel of a dress. I tried to buy it from her, but she refused. Something about her uncle's will. I'm an expert, you see, at restoring old costumes—although I must say, that gown is in remarkable condition. It doesn't need any work."

So Wellington had tried to buy Diana's dress. Everything he said seemed to bring him closer to the crimes. "What about Amanda Hyde-Porter?" Nancy asked.

"It was a real pity about that manuscript." Wellington gave a heavy sigh. "I spotted it just as it came on the market, but Amanda beat me to it. It was a treasure." He scowled at Nancy. "If you're thinking *I* put a torch to that script, forget it. I wanted it, to be sure. But I would never harm an antique just to get even with somebody. That would be madness. And now, if you'll excuse me, I have work to do."

As she preceded Bess and George out onto the sunny street, Nancy tried to decide what she thought of Peter Wellington. Was he putting on an act? It was hard to imagine him setting fire to anything—especially an antique—but there was something almost fanatical about him. And that bothered her.

At least he had given her a new lead—Sheik Hassan Karim Abdullah—and a question to answer. Who was the bearded young man she had seen leaving Wellington's shop? And what was his interest in this case?

"Well, here we are," Nancy announced a few hours later, swinging the white Lincoln into the palm-bordered drive that led up to Diana Normandy's Beverly Hills mansion.

Bess leaned forward and nervously scrutinized herself in the car's mirror. "Do you think we're dressed okay for the party?" she asked. Back at the hotel after their morning in Venice, she had changed into a peach-colored dress that emphasized her curvy figure and had fastened her shoulder-length blond hair back with gold clips.

"You and Nancy both look terrific," George said. George looked great herself in a lipstick-red jumpsuit and red sandals.

Nancy checked her makeup quickly. She'd chosen a pair of white linen pants and a gold top that brought out the bright highlights in her red-blond hair. "Okay, gang," she said, getting out of the car. "Let's get to work."

Diana's house is even more imposing than Amanda's, Nancy thought as a uniformed maid answered the doorbell and let them in. Outside, it looked like a transplanted Southern plantation house, with tall white pillars spaced across the front. Inside, it was crammed with artwork —paintings, sculpture, books, costumes.

"Isn't this a fabulous place?" Diana asked, rushing toward them. She was wearing a long black frizzy wig with a leopard-printed minidress cinched in at the waist with a heavy gold belt. She giggled. "I inherited it all from my uncle Samuel. If it were up to me, I'd sell all this stupid old junk in a minute and spend it all on parties. Unfortunately, my uncle's will forbids me to sell any—"

"So *there* you are, Diana," Amanda said, interrupting and running up behind her friend. She turned to Nancy. "Oh, hi, Nancy. I'm glad you're here." She lowered her voice. "The dressmaker delivered the substitute gown a little while ago. Both of the dresses are upstairs in the costume display room. And you don't need to worry. The locks on the display cases are burglar-proof. Come on up—we'll show you."

Nancy and her friends followed Diana and Amanda up the stairs to a large paneled room whose walls were lined with glass cases displaying costumes of all periods. On one side of the room, French doors were open. They led onto a balcony that overlooked a lush green garden and an enormous swimming pool. Already, maids in black uniforms were laying out a lavish buffet on tables beside the pool, and a band was setting up.

"Look, Nancy!" George exclaimed, pointing

to a gown hung on a dress form in front of a closed case.

Nancy took a deep breath. "So *this* is the Flame," she said admiringly. The bare-shouldered gown was made of flame-colored satin with a subtle pattern woven into it. It had a high waistline and short, puffed sleeves. An ornate gold brooch, shaped like a crown, was fastened to the bodice. "It's beautiful," she added. "And in such good condition! You'd never know it's almost two hundred years old."

"Actually, it's not," Amanda corrected her. "That's the copy. *This* is the Flame." She unlocked a display case and took out another gown draped on a dress form.

"Why," Bess exclaimed, her eyes widening, "it's identical!"

"Of course," Amanda said with a laugh. "That's the point, isn't it? We want the extortionist to mistake the copy for the original."

"But this dress doesn't look two hundred years old either," George said, fingering the real Flame's fabric. "It looks brand—"

Outside, the musicians crashed into a rock tune and drowned out her words completely.

"Do I have to hang around up here, Amanda?" Diana asked, raising her voice. "People will be arriving any minute now, and I want to—"

"Oh, go on," Amanda said a little impatiently. She turned to Nancy. "That reminds me—

there's something I have to attend to, Nancy. Would you mind putting the original dress away for me?"

Nancy looked around the room. "We're going to hide it in one of the locked cases," she said. "But we'll leave the copy out in plain sight."

"Whatever you say. You're in charge." Amanda handed Nancy the keys. "Let me know if you need anything, and I'll check in with you when I get a chance. Good luck!" With a quick smile, she followed Diana out of the room.

Bess leaned forward and touched the Flame reverently. "Isn't it beautiful?" she asked, awe in her voice. "Just imagine—the empress Josephine wore this very dress herself."

"It *is* lovely," George said. "With the shimmering fabric in that color, I see why it's called the Flame. I can't get over how new it looks."

"Obviously it's been very well preserved," Nancy said. "It was probably in a museum somewhere until Diana's uncle bought it."

"I'd love to try it on," Bess said, still looking wistfully at the Flame. "But I'd need to lose another five pounds. Actually, it's about your size, George." She turned to Nancy. "Do you suppose it'd be all right if George tried it on?"

"That's an antique! It's irreplaceable. You could ruin it if you tried it on," Nancy said.

"I don't agree," said George, gently fingering the sleeve of the dress. "The fabric looks as though it's in perfect condition. And it also

39

looks as though it would fit me perfectly. Oh, come on, Nan! Just this once! I'll never get another chance to wear something an empress wore."

Nancy reached out and touched the fabric herself. George was right—it *did* seem to be in perfect condition. "Okay," she finally said. "But only for a minute. And please, please, be careful!"

It took only a minute for George to step out of her jumpsuit and pull the Flame over her head. There was a long mirror on one side of the room, and she turned around in front of it, adjusting the gold brooch on the bodice.

"Oh, George," Bess said in an awestruck voice. "You look just like an empress! You're beautiful!"

Nancy stared at her friend. In Empress Josephine's gown, shoulders back, head held high and proud, George *did* look like a queen. It was a remarkable transformation. "I think you missed your calling, George," Nancy said with a laugh. "You should have been an empress. Okay, you guys, let's put the dress away for safekeeping right now. I'd never forgive myself if anything happened to—"

George took one more turn in front of the mirror. Then she stopped, a puzzled look on her face. Her fingers went to the golden crown at the bodice. "You know, something seems odd about

this dress, Nancy," she said. "Something—"
And then she let out a terrified shriek.

Nancy whirled around. There was a soft hiss, and two wings of bright flame flared where the bodice met the skirt of the Empire-style gown. In an instant the fire had ignited the bodice, and the sleeves and the skirt were veiled in a curtain of smoke.

In another few seconds George would be a human torch!

Chapter

Five

WITHOUT AN INSTANT'S hesitation, Nancy spun George around and threw her to the floor. "Roll, George!" she shouted. "It's your only chance! Roll!" While she was barking orders at George, Nancy picked up one corner of the oriental rug covering the floor and ran with it toward George. With one enormous tug, she lifted it high and covered her friend, beating out the last licks of tiny flame.

George staggered to her feet. She was groggy from the smoke and in shock. Lurching wildly, she went out on the balcony for some fresh air. She fell against the railing and continued to fall—headlong over the rail—straight into the pool twenty-five feet below. A split second later, Nancy followed.

The water closed over Nancy's head, but she surfaced quickly, gulping great lungfuls of air. George! Where was George? She didn't see her anywhere.

"There she is!" a man yelled from the edge of the pool.

"I'll get her!" another man shouted. Nancy heard a splash as somebody dived in.

"Nancy!" Bess cried from the balcony. "I think she's unconscious."

Nancy heaved herself out of the pool. On the other side a crowd was gathering as a man in the water was supporting George's limp body. Nancy dashed around the pool and helped to pull George from the water.

"Artificial respiration!" a woman gasped. "Give her artificial respiration!"

"No," the man answered. "She's breathing."

Gently Nancy touched George's forehead. She was unconscious and breathing rapidly; there was a lump the size of an egg on her forehead. The Empress's Flame, charred and wet, clung to her lithe frame.

"Let's get her inside and warm her up," a man's voice said. "She's in shock."

Nancy looked up, amazed. The voice belonged to the same bearded young man she had seen coming out of Peter Wellington's shop earlier that morning—and he was dripping wet. He had jumped into the pool to rescue George.

Carefully, he scooped her up and carried her toward the house.

"I'll take care of her," Nancy told the crowd of people who'd gathered around the pool. "I'm working for Diana. You all go back and have a good time." She didn't want everyone trooping along behind them.

Diana was waiting for them in the den. "What happened?" she demanded as the stranger gingerly put George down on a sofa. "She's all wet! Why did you put her on my silk sofa?" Then her eyes widened as she saw the dress. "The Flame! Oh no! Is it—?"

"How is she, Nancy?" Bess asked, dashing into the room with a blanket in her arms and Amanda on her heels.

"What's going on?" Amanda asked. "I saw a body fall into the—" Her hand flew to her mouth when she saw George. "Oh no!"

Nancy nodded grimly. "It's the Flame, I'm afraid. I can't tell you how sorry I am. George was wearing it when it suddenly went up in—" She stopped. George's eyelids were flickering open. "George, are you all right?" Nancy asked.

George choked and struggled to sit up. "I—I think so," she said in a dazed voice. "I'm just—dizzy, that's all."

"You've got a few burns. I think we'd better get you to the hospital," Nancy told her. "The lump on your head doesn't look serious, but it wouldn't hurt to have it examined, just to rule out concussion. And we do have to see how badly you've been burned."

"I'll take her." It was Brent Kincaid. Nancy hadn't seen him come in, but now he was standing next to Amanda. "My car's right outside."

"Good," Nancy said. "But first we need to get her out of that wet dress. I don't think she's so badly burned that we have to leave it on her."

After everyone had left the room, Nancy and Bess carefully peeled George out of the dress and wrapped her in the blanket. "Nan, I should have listened to you. The Flame is ruined," George said, staring woefully at the charred and tattered dress. "Look, even the brooch is gone."

"It's my fault too," Bess said. "I feel like such a— What are you doing, Nancy?"

Nancy was bent over the dress, examining it closely. "I'm trying to figure out how the fire started," she said. "I mean, this whole thing is crazy. The flames just leaped out of nowhere!"

"Brent's brought the car to the front door," Amanda said, walking back into the room with Diana.

"Okay, we're coming," Nancy replied. "It would probably be a good idea to take the Flame back upstairs and lock it up."

Amanda nodded. "I'll do it right away," she promised. She gestured to the patio. "But first I think I'd better let everybody know that things are under control."

45

"Of course," Nancy said absently. She turned to Diana. "What can I say? I'm so sorry this happened. It was completely unprofessional of me to let George try on the dress. I—I wish I could—"

"Well, I am upset, naturally, but there's no use thinking about it now," Diana cut in. "I'll just have to live with it, I guess. You'd better get George to the hospital, and we can talk about this later."

"All right," Nancy said bleakly.

It was several hours later when Nancy got back to Diana's mansion. Amanda met her at the front door. "How's George?" she asked.

"The doctor says she's going to be okay," Nancy said. "She was lucky. She got out of it with only a few burns and a headache. Bess took her back to the hotel in a taxi." She paused for a moment and listened to the loud music and voices from the back of the house. "It sounds as if the party's still going on."

Amanda smiled. "Diana's parties *always* go on—and on and on." Then she grew serious. "I suppose you want to look at the remains of the Flame. It's upstairs, with the copy."

Nancy nodded and followed Amanda up to the display room. "There must be *some* clue to what started the fire," Nancy said. "I expected to find some trace of an incendiary device when

I looked at the dress earlier. But I didn't see a thing."

As they reached the door of the room, Diana joined them. Nancy turned to her. "Do you have the key to this room, Diana?"

"Oh, the room's not locked," Amanda said. She pushed on the door. It swung open.

"Don't you think it *should* be locked?" Nancy asked.

Diana looked confused. "Well, I—"

"We didn't really think we needed to lock it," Amanda interrupted. "After all, the arsonist has already done his work, hasn't he? The Flame's destroyed."

Nancy sighed. Don't remind me, she thought. She knew it would be a long time before she could forgive herself for what had happened. "I suppose you're right," she said.

The room was dark. Nancy switched on the lights—and what she saw stopped her in her tracks. The dress forms were there, but they were both empty.

Behind Nancy, Amanda gasped and Diana gave a loud shriek. "The gowns have been stolen!" Diana cried. "The Flame is gone!"

Chapter
Six

Outside, the musicians had taken a break, and Diana's voice was loud in the silence. "There's a thief in my house! I'm going to call the police!"

"But I—I don't understand," Amanda said, her forehead wrinkled. "Who would steal a damaged antique gown? And what would anyone want with a copy?"

"Obviously," Nancy said, "the thief didn't want anybody to examine that dress. He might have taken the copy just to confuse the issue. Or he might not have been sure which one was real. And, of course, hiding the dresses also hides any clue to how the Flame caught on fire."

Suddenly the sound of a shuffling step in the hallway caught her attention. Nancy stepped swiftly and silently to the door and yanked it open.

Outside, bent over slightly as though he'd been listening, stood the bearded, good-looking man she had seen coming out of Wellington's shop—the same one who had pulled George out of the pool.

"Oh, hello," the young man said mildly, straightening up. He brushed his sun-streaked brown hair back with his fingers and smiled. "I thought I saw you come upstairs. I just wanted to ask about your friend George. Is she all right?"

Nancy stared at him suspiciously. He returned her gaze, his blue-green eyes steady. She was positive that he'd been eavesdropping outside the door. Why? What was his connection to the case? "The doctor said she'd be okay with a little rest," she said. "Uh, what did you say your name was?"

"Oh, Chad!" Diana exclaimed, dashing into the hall. "I understand that *you're* the one who jumped into the pool to save Nancy's friend from drowning." She fluttered her long eyelashes flirtatiously. "Chad Bannister is my new neighbor," she said.

Chad grinned at Nancy, and a dimple formed in his cheek. He *was* gorgeous, Nancy thought. "Could you tell your friend that I'll give her a call this evening? Whenever I save a girl from drowning, I like to check up on her."

"Miss Normandy?" A maid was standing in the doorway. "The police are here."

"Oh! Send them up," Diana said. "Nancy, we called the police. It's not that I don't think you're— I just wanted to call in the police for the record."

"It's a formality for the insurance company," Amanda interrupted. "After discussing it, we definitely want you to stay on the case, Nancy— so don't worry about that."

I'll try not to, Nancy thought.

George put down the telephone beside the sofa in their hotel suite. Her cheeks were pink, her dark eyes sparkling. "Is Chad Bannister really that good-looking, Nancy?" she asked.

"What's the matter, George?" Bess teased. "Can't you remember?"

George touched the lump on her head, looking frustrated. "That's the funny part," she said. "I can't remember anything from the time I put on the dress until I woke up on the sofa."

"I know your head still hurts," Nancy said, sitting down beside George, "but I'm sure the police and the insurance company need to question you. It would be helpful if you could try to remember something."

"What did the police find when they came to investigate?" Bess asked, pulling the tab on a diet soda.

Nancy shook her head. "Nothing. They took

statements from us and poked around for a little while. Then they left. Maybe they don't have to work as hard on cases like this when an insurance company has to do so much work." She glanced at George. "What did Chad have to say?"

George threw Nancy a sidelong look. "Oh, just that he'd like to take me out. I might be tempted. What would you think if I went out with him tomorrow night?"

Nancy ran her fingers through her hair. "Actually, George, I think it'd be a good idea if you went out with him. Maybe you can find out what his connection is to all this." She shook her head. "I mean, it's got to be more than a coincidence that he showed up at Wellington's asking questions just a couple of hours before Diana's gown was torched."

"Oh, so you want me to spend my date playing detective again?" George said, raising her eyebrows.

"You got it," Nancy told her with a grin. They were both remembering Nancy's last case, *Rich and Dangerous,* when George had gone out with a good-looking suspect to find out some vital information. "After all, we're here to work, aren't we?"

She leaned back on the sofa. "I've been thinking about our suspect list. Brent seems to be off the list, since he doesn't have any motive. Before I left the party, I asked him if it was possible that either Amanda or Diana might be involved in this somehow."

Bess took a sip of her soda. "What did he say?"

"He just pointed out that both Diana and Amanda have plenty of money. I had to agree that Amanda doesn't seem to have a motive. She could have sold the manuscript for more than she'll get from the insurance company. And, of course, Diana has money to burn. You can't give parties the way she does unless you're—"

Just then the telephone rang. On the other end, Preston Talbot greeted her, saying he was sorry to bother her on Sunday night. Then he got down to business.

"I understand that you've met Elaine Ellsworth, who works for our insurance company," Mr. Talbot said. "Well, she asked me if she could question you—something about a gown that her company has insured. She said you'd know what it was about. Would it be too inconvenient to meet with her tonight?"

Nancy said, "No, it wouldn't be." They decided to meet in Mr. Talbot's office since he was there working.

Mr. Talbot paused, then asked Nancy about the progress she was making on the case.

"Well, we're getting *somewhere,*" Nancy told him. "We've learned that our suspect could be somebody with a fixation about Napoleon. He

—or she—has made extortion attempts three times in the last two weeks, and each time he's destroyed a valuable antique."

Mr. Talbot gave a short laugh. "Well," he said, "whoever he is, I hope he's met his Waterloo. Good luck, Nancy."

"Who was it, Nancy?" Bess asked as Nancy sat staring at the phone.

"It was Preston Talbot," Nancy said. "Elaine Ellsworth wants to talk to me about the Flame. Apparently, her company insured it." She frowned. "But I can't figure out how she found out about the arson so fast—and on a Sunday night!"

Nancy's question was answered ten minutes later when she met Elaine Ellsworth in Mr. Talbot's office. Ms. Ellsworth was sitting behind Mr. Talbot's large desk, reading the police report.

"I apologize for calling you on a Sunday," she said, "but when I'm working on an arson case I like to move fast—before the trail gets cold." She took Nancy in with her cool gray eyes. "I understand from the police report that you were at Diana Normandy's house when the Empress's Flame was destroyed and that you were with Ms. Normandy when she discovered that the remains of the gown were missing." She handed the report to Nancy. "Do you have anything to add to the statement that you made to the police?"

Nancy read it over and told Ms. Ellsworth what she had seen. "There is one other thing you should know, since you're working on the arson case here at the hotel. I'm a private detective. Mr. Talbot asked me to—"

Ms. Ellsworth cut her off. "I know. He's explained why you're here." She leaned forward intently. "I must say, Ms. Drew, that I find it a little curious that you have become involved with a *second* arson case so soon after your arrival here."

Nancy met her gaze. "It's not curious at all," she said with a little shrug. "I was simply following up on a lead to an earlier arson—the burning of Amanda Hyde-Porter's manuscript of *Napoleon and Josephine*. As I told the police, that's how I met Diana Normandy."

Elaine Ellsworth put down the report. "I see," she said. "Well, I have no wish to interfere, Ms. Drew. But I must remind you that the penalty for withholding evidence in an arson investigation is quite—"

Nancy sat up straight. She was furious but determined not to show it. "I'm not withholding any evidence," she said steadily.

"Good." Ms. Ellsworth smiled, but the smile didn't quite reach her eyes. "Then I'm sure you'll keep me posted on the progress of your investigation, won't you?"

* * *

It was Monday morning, and the girls were on their way to Marina del Rey to question Professor Nicole Ronsarde. Nancy had just finished telling her friends about Elaine Ellsworth's questioning.

"It almost sounds as if Ms. Ellsworth suspects *you*, Nancy," Bess said.

"I think she does," Nancy responded, pulling Mr. Talbot's Lincoln into the oceanside parking lot at the marina. "At the very least, she thinks I'm withholding information." She shook her head. "I don't think it's a serious problem, but it could slow up my investigation."

"I've never been on a houseboat before," George remarked as they walked along the pier past luxurious teak-and-chrome yachts and fancy houseboats. "I wonder what it would be like to live on one."

"Cramped," Nancy said with a laugh. "And you'd probably have plenty of sea gulls for company." She pointed to a large cedar-shingled houseboat at the end of the pier. A small forest of ferns was growing on the deck, and three gulls perched on the railing. "This must be it."

Their knock was answered by a small, gray-haired, bright-eyed woman dressed in green. Two white Persian cats with gold collars wound themselves around her ankles, and she was holding a third cat in her arms.

"Hello," the woman said. She had a heavy French accent. "What can I do for you?"

"My name is Nancy Drew," Nancy began, "and these are my associates, Bess Marvin and George Fayne. We'd like to talk to you about a manuscript that belonged to Amanda Hyde-Porter—a manuscript that was unfortunately burned a couple of weeks ago. The manuscript was called *Napoleon and Josephine,* and it was written by—"

But Nancy didn't get to finish her sentence. "Amanda! That lying wretch!" Professor Ronsarde shouted so loudly that the sea gulls flapped away. Frightened, the cat jumped out of her arms and scurried across the deck. "Amanda is the one who should be torched. She stole the *Napoleon.* It was mine!"

Chapter

Seven

NANCY STARED AT Professor Ronsarde in shock. "Amanda stole it from you? You mean the manuscript was yours?"

The professor opened the door. "Come in," she said. "You must hear the whole story immediately—the truth this time."

As the girls trooped into the houseboat, they looked around in surprise. It wasn't cramped at all. A window covered one wall of the living room, opening out to a view of the ocean. On another wall was a fireplace. And it was obvious that the professor was a book lover, for books were everywhere—lining the walls, stacked on the floor, spilling off tables. Cats were everywhere, too. Nancy counted at least four.

"You see," Professor Ronsarde said as the

girls sat down, "I can never resist a good book. Books are my life. I live for books." A gray Persian cat jumped off a shelf and onto her lap. "And for my cats, of course," she added. "Hello, Voltaire." She began to stroke the cat, crooning softly into its ear.

"You had planned to add *Napoleon and Josephine* to your collection?" Nancy prompted her.

"Yes." The professor looked up, her eyes dark. "In fact, I had identified the manuscript as the original, written in the author's own hand. This is what gave it such great value. Then, just as I was preparing to make the purchase, Amanda Hyde-Porter swooped in and bought it for double my offer. She did it to spite me!"

"Oh, I see," George said. "So that's why you're upset with her."

Professor Ronsarde straightened up in her chair, and her voice began to rise. "Yes, that is why! I tell you, Amanda is to blame for all that has happened. If she had not cheated me out of the *Napoleon,* it would still be safe. It would have been mine!"

Nancy frowned. "But why did you want the manuscript in the first place? I understand that you aren't exactly a fan of Napoleon's."

Professor Ronsarde stared at her blankly. "Who gave you that idea?" she asked. "Napoleon was one of France's greatest leaders."

The girls exchanged glances. "But Amanda said—" Bess began.

"Amanda!" the professor exclaimed. "She is a liar as well as a thief!"

Nancy stood up. "Do you have any information about how the manuscript burned?" she asked.

The professor shook her head. "All I know is that it was a terrible deed," she said mournfully. "Such a sad thing, to burn such a valuable piece of history."

For a moment the room was silent. Then Nancy took out a piece of paper and scribbled some numbers on it. "These are the telephone numbers," she said, "for our hotel room and our car phone. You'll call us, won't you," she added, "if you think of anything else we ought to know?"

A Siamese cat jumped from the back of the sofa onto Professor Ronsarde's shoulder. "I will," the professor said, tucking the paper into her pocket. She glowered furiously. "And if you see Amanda, tell her for me that I will find a way to get even with her for what she has done!"

"Whew!" George said as the girls climbed back into the Lincoln. "What a character! Book lover, cat lover—"

"And Napoleon lover," Bess broke in. "I wonder why Amanda lied about her."

Nancy started the car. "We don't know which

one is lying," she pointed out. "Obviously there's bad blood between the two of them. Amanda could be lying to make trouble for a former professor she doesn't like. Or Professor Ronsarde could be lying to cover her tracks." She frowned. "Still, it's hard for me to believe that the professor is responsible. I think she's too much of a book lover to burn a valuable manuscript."

"Unless Amanda's right and the professor really hates Napoleon," George said. "Maybe the arsonist's real motive is to destroy anything connected to or about Napoleon."

"I don't know, George," Nancy said. She pulled out of the parking lot and down the palm-lined highway.

"Where to now, Nancy?" Bess asked.

"Kincaid Studios is only a few miles from here," Nancy said. "I think we ought to pay Brent a visit and find out more about the sheik who lost the Napoleon miniature in that poker game."

"Terrific!" Bess crowed, clapping her hands. "Hollywood, here we come!"

"Nancy!" Brent Kincaid turned away from the filming crew he was watching and walked toward the three girls. "What a pleasant surprise! You're just in time to see—"

"Fire in the hole!" came a shout from across the set.

Behind Brent there was a giant explosion. As Nancy and her friends watched in openmouthed horror, the wall of one of the buildings on the set behind him collapsed in a cloud of smoke. A giant fireball sent waves of scorching heat over them.

"That building just blew up!" Bess exclaimed in horror.

Brent turned for a look. "So it did," he said calmly.

"But why don't they *do* something about it?" Bess asked.

Brent laughed. "They *are* doing something about it, my dear. They're filming it. The building isn't a real one, of course, and the explosion was part of a scene. The whole thing is part of the illusion of making movies." He smiled a little patronizingly at Bess. "I see that it was a successful illusion—at least as far as you're concerned."

Bess blushed. "Well, it looks like a real fire to me," she said defensively. "I don't know that much about making movies."

"That's something we ought to take care of right now," Brent said. He waved, and a young man came hurrying over. "Tom, these girls have never visited a Hollywood studio. Would you see that they're given the grand tour? And make sure that they get over to Soundstage B. I think they'll be interested in the rock singer who's filming this afternoon—Michael Seaton."

61

"Yes, sir, Mr. Kincaid," Tom said.

"Is it okay, Nan?" Bess asked, her eyes sparkling. "You know how much I love Michael Seaton."

"Sure," Nancy said. "You and George go while I talk to Brent." When Bess and George had left, she turned to him. "That was a spectacular explosion. Do you do stunts like that often?"

Brent shrugged. "Often enough. Of course, I don't have anything to do with that end of the business. Blowing things up isn't exactly my department." He grinned at her. "Walk with me—I'm on my way to my office. You did want to talk to me, didn't you?" Brent asked.

"Actually, I did come to ask you a couple of questions," Nancy said as Brent led her into a large, elegant office with walnut paneling and a huge built-in TV screen on one wall.

Brent sat down at his desk, and Nancy took the chair across from him. "Ask away," Brent said, leaning back comfortably.

"Is it true that you didn't actually buy the Napoleon miniature—that you won it in a poker game?" Nancy asked.

Brent smiled sheepishly. "Yes, that's exactly how I did get it. Kind of embarrassing, isn't it? Abdullah lost a lot of money, and I decided that I'd rather have the miniature than the cash."

"How did he take the loss?" Nancy asked. "Was he angry?"

"Yes," Brent said simply. "Nobody likes to lose. I think he was pretty attached to that miniature, too. Maybe I shouldn't have done it."

"Do you think he was angry enough to try to get even with you?"

Brent sat up straighter and looked at her. "You know," he said thoughtfully, "that never occurred to me. I suppose it is a possibility. He could have done it out of spite and glossed it over with a phony extortion note. Or maybe he really thought he'd get some money out of me." Then he shook his head. "But, no, we're friends. I can't believe he'd do that."

"And there doesn't seem to be any connection between the sheik and the other two crimes," Nancy pointed out. "Still, it's worth following up. Maybe we'll find a connection. Can you give me his address?"

"I don't have it here," Brent said. "I'll call you tomorrow. Any other questions, Nancy?"

"Just one. About Diana's dress. Do you know who might have burned it or how it might have been done?"

Brent looked perplexed and shrugged. "Wish I did," he said. "I still think Wellington's the guy to go after. He seems just crazy enough to torch something he couldn't have for himself. And Diana did tell me that he was really upset when she wouldn't sell her gown to him. Now, if you could establish a connection between him and Amanda's manuscript, I think you'd have it made."

I guess I'll talk to Wellington again, Nancy thought.

"As for how it could have been done," Brent added, "I don't have a clue. The insurance company's really baffled by this thing, too. There are no clues."

"That's true, unfortunately," Nancy said. "And without clues, I have to fall back on motive and opportunity. And I'm not getting anywhere there, either."

Brent leaned forward. "Could we talk about something a little more pleasant for a sec? Preston called this morning to remind me about the costume gala at the hotel on Friday night. You know about it, of course."

Nancy nodded.

"Anyway, it occurred to me that if you and your friends are still in town, you might like to go. And if you do, you'll need costumes. Well, Kincaid Studios has a terrific costume department. You can be anybody you want: a Southern belle, a samurai, Cinderella—you name it, the costume is yours."

"Great!" Nancy said enthusiastically. "I'm sure Bess and George will be excited too."

Suddenly the door opened, and Bess and George burst into the office. "Michael Seaton just autographed his new tape for me!" Bess bubbled. She spun around, clutching a cassette.

"I can't believe it! Michael Seaton's autograph!"

It was late afternoon by the time the girls got back to the hotel. George left for her date with Chad, and now Bess was lying on the floor listening to Michael Seaton's new tape. Mark Thompson had to fly that night, so Bess was on her own. Nancy had just sat down to go over her notes on this complicated, frustrating case when she was interrupted by a knock at the door. A bellboy handed her an envelope, which she instantly opened.

" 'I'd like to talk to you again, Ms. Drew,' " she read. " 'Come to Mr. Talbot's office as soon as possible.' " The note was signed by Elaine Ellsworth.

Nancy frowned. That woman had a lot of nerve. This sounded like a command. Nancy felt like not going—after all, it was seven o'clock. But her curiosity won out, and soon she found herself seated in Mr. Talbot's office opposite Ms. Ellsworth.

Elaine Ellsworth tapped a pencil against the desk, studying Nancy. For a long moment she didn't say anything.

Finally she spoke. "Miss Drew, I think it's time for us to be honest with each other. I've identified the arsonist."

Nancy blinked. So, the case was over. For a moment Nancy felt a little jealous that the case had been solved without her help. But she pushed the feeling aside. The important thing was that Mr. Talbot was off the hook and the reputation of the hotel was safe.

"I'm glad to hear that you've solved the case," she said. "And I'm sure Mr. Talbot is delighted."

At that moment Nancy's eye fell on a notepad at the corner of Mr. Talbot's desk. The notepaper was gray, with a distinctive red border—the same paper that the extortion notes had been written on!

Watching Nancy, Elaine Ellsworth smiled triumphantly. "Ah, I see that *you've* made the connection too."

Nancy looked up. "What connection?"

"Why, the connection to your employer, of course. Preston Talbot—he's the arsonist!"

Chapter

Eight

PRESTON TALBOT!" NANCY said, not trusting her ears. "Where's your evidence? And what kind of motive could he possibly have?"

"Motive? Why, the oldest motive in the book," Elaine Ellsworth said. She sat back in the chair, her eyes on Nancy's. "Money. Preston Talbot needs the million dollars that he tried to extort from Brent Kincaid. He tried extortion with Amanda Hyde-Porter *and* with Diana Normandy. But he didn't count on the fact that his victims would refuse to pay, so he had to destroy the objects."

"But that's all conjecture," Nancy objected angrily. "Where's your evidence?"

"The motive *is* the evidence, Ms. Drew. Mr. Talbot is in desperate need of money. You may not know it, but this hotel is in the red. He needs every cent he can get. And besides . . ."

Ms. Ellsworth leaned forward again and reached for the notepad without taking her eyes from Nancy's. "Do you recognize this?" she asked, holding up the pad.

Nancy swallowed hard. "I-I'm not sure," she said, stalling for time.

"Well, I am," Elaine Ellsworth answered in a satisfied tone. "It's the same paper that was used for the extortion notes. It came from Mr. Talbot's desk. And if that's not enough . . ."

She reached for a sheet of ledger paper covered with rows of figures. "I suppose you know that the hotel vault contained the week's cash receipts, well over a quarter of a million dollars —or at least that's what they're claiming."

Nancy nodded. What was this all about?

"We've gone over the records of the hotel's various accounts," Ms. Ellsworth said, running her finger down the ledger page. "We don't believe there was that much money in the vault. In fact, we're not certain that there was any money in it at all." She fixed her eyes on Nancy again. "It's possible that what was burned was just paper—something that would leave ashes that *looked* like burned bills."

"But that doesn't connect Mr. Talbot to this case," Nancy protested.

"No, not by itself," Ms. Ellsworth replied.

There was a slight smile on her lips. "But when you put all the pieces together—"

"Ms. Ellsworth," Nancy interrupted, "if Mr. Talbot is really responsible, why would he use his own notepaper? Why extort money only from people with Napoleonic relics? And why bring *me* in to investigate the case?"

Ms. Ellsworth arched her brows. *"You* tell *me,* Ms. Drew," she responded softly. "You tell me."

Nancy stood up. Was Ms. Ellsworth trying to suggest that Nancy and Mr. Talbot were in it together? This was ridiculous! There was no point in trying to reason with the insurance investigator. She had made up her mind. "If you're finished," Nancy said, "I have work to do."

Ms. Ellsworth looked startled, as if she'd expected more of a reaction. "Yes, I'm finished," she said. "For the moment." She gave Nancy a stern look. "But make sure that your 'work' doesn't get in the way of this investigation."

"They found the notepad on Mr. Talbot's desk?" Bess asked, sitting cross-legged on her bed. She was wearing a pink nightshirt and digging a fork into a bowl of shrimp salad that she'd ordered from room service.

Nancy picked up her hairbrush and nodded,

frowning. "I just talked to him a minute ago on the phone. Of course, he knows that Elaine Ellsworth suspects him. He says that the notepad does belong to him, but that anybody could have taken paper from it. Lots of people have access to his office. The hotel does have money problems, as does the airline, he says. In fact, if you just look at motive alone, Mr. Talbot is a likely suspect. And of course, if he's charged it'll be all over the newspapers. Then he'll really be in trouble. Which means we've got to work fast to keep him from being formally accused."

"You don't think he did it?"

"No way," Nancy replied emphatically. "He wouldn't try to bail out his hotel through extortion or by faking receipts. I'll stake my reputation on it."

Bess speared a shrimp. "You know, Nan," she mused, "this case is really crazy. A portrait that burns up in a locked vault, a gown that bursts into flame with George in it, a manuscript that's torched under a guard's nose—" She looked up, her eyes round. "Do you think there *could* be something supernatural going on? I mean, like a curse or something?"

Nancy smiled. "No, I don't think there's something like a curse," she said gently. "Our problem is that we don't know how the fires start. And even though we've got four suspects, none of them is connected to all three of the cases."

"Four suspects?" Bess began to count on her fingers. "Peter Wellington, Professor Ronsarde, and Sheik Abdullah—who's the fourth?"

Nancy stopped brushing and looked at Bess. "Chad Bannister."

"Chad? You mean George's date tonight?" Bess frowned. "How could he be involved?"

"I don't know," Nancy said. "But he was asking Wellington questions, and then he showed up at Diana's party—just in time for the Flame to burn. He's tied in somehow."

At that moment there was noise in the living room. Putting her finger to her lips to caution Bess, Nancy went to the bedroom door and opened it wide enough to peek through. It was George, and she was saying good night to Chad —with a lingering kiss.

"What is it, Nancy?" Bess asked worriedly.

"George," Nancy told her with a grin. "She's winding up her detective work with Chad."

In another moment George came into the bedroom, her eyes sparkling and her cheeks flushed pink.

"Okay, George," Bess said meaningfully. "How was your date?"

She smiled. "Fantastic," she said. "We started out at this wonderful little sushi bar—"

Bess wrinkled her nose. "Ugh," she said.

"Raw fish. I'll take mine cooked, thank you."
She speared another shrimp.

"Then we went to a funny little Italian restaurant and had ravioli, and then we went to a Greek place to dance."

"That's not a date," Bess protested. "That's a world tour."

"Did you find out anything about Chad?" Nancy asked.

George frowned. "You mean, did I carry out my detective assignment?"

"Well, something like that," Nancy admitted with a grin.

"He's from La Jolla," George said. "He graduated from UCLA. He's got a boat at Marina del Rey, and he's just moved into a new house in Beverly Hills. He's a terrific dancer, a great conversationalist, and one of the best-looking guys I've ever met." She looked defensive. "Is that what you're after?"

Nancy sighed. With her logical mind and her athletic prowess, George was usually a great help. But sometimes she managed to get herself emotionally involved in a case, and when she did she usually went overboard. Nancy hoped fervently that this wasn't going to be one of those times.

"One more thing," Nancy said. "Did you happen to find out how he supports himself? How can he afford a yacht and a house in Beverly Hills?"

"He made some good investments," George said briefly. She began changing. "I'm really tired. Do you think we could postpone the rest of the questions until tomorrow?"

Bess sighed as she sat beside Nancy in the front seat of the white Lincoln on Tuesday morning. "This view is gorgeous. Why do people complain about L.A.?"

"But this isn't L.A.," George objected from the backseat. "It's Malibu."

"Wherever it is," Bess said, "it's heavenly. Just look at that ocean!"

Nancy quickly glanced to her left as she drove. The cliff on the side of the road fell away steeply to the rocks below, where the surf thundered in heaving white billows. "The view may be beautiful," she said, "but this road certainly is dangerous." She slowed down to let another driver pass her. "I wish people wouldn't pass on these blind curves. You can't see what's coming."

"How far is it to the sheik's?" George asked.

"Another three or four miles," Nancy replied. "So far Brent's directions have been good." Brent Kincaid had called that morning with the phone number and address, and the sheik was expecting them at eleven sharp. Nancy felt a little nervous. She'd certainly never interviewed a sheik in a Malibu mansion before!

"Look at that view!" Bess marveled again.

"I *can't* look, Bess," Nancy said testily. "If I do, we'll all end up in the drink." She glanced in the rearview mirror. A small blue sports car had been behind them for the last ten minutes. She'd slowed a couple of times, hoping it would pass, but the driver had hung behind, and Nancy had momentarily forgotten about it. Now, however, the car had caught up with them again. It was practically hugging their bumper. "I wish that driver would make up his mind to pass," Nancy said.

George turned to glance out the rear window. "Looks as if he heard you," she said.

The blue car was speeding up and swinging to the left. Nancy couldn't tell whether the driver and the passenger were men or women. The car's smoked-glass windows were so dark that all she could see was the outline of two people. She turned her attention back to her driving. They were coming into a particularly nasty hairpin curve, and she needed to focus all her concentration on the road ahead.

But as the blue sports car pulled alongside them, Nancy glanced quickly to the side. Someone in a rubber Dracula mask was leaning out the window. He had a large cup in his hand, which he tossed at Nancy's windshield. In an instant the glass was completely covered with a thick black liquid, like engine oil. Nancy couldn't see a thing! The car began to lurch out of control.

"Nancy!" George screamed. "Watch out! We're going over the cliff!"

Chapter

Nine

"HANG ON, EVERYBODY!" Nancy yelled, gently pumping the brakes.

The curve was littered with loose gravel. Nancy felt the car skidding and sliding sideways toward the edge of the cliff. She eased the steering wheel in the direction of the skid, trying not to panic—and hoping to regain control before they crashed through the low guard rail. Then, just as it seemed they were going to spin off the road and crash onto the rocks below, Nancy turned the wheel and the car responded. She swung it into a scenic overlook.

George whistled. "That was close!"

"What were they trying to do?" Bess demanded when she caught her breath. "Kill us?"

Nancy fell back against the seat and stared at the windshield. "It sure seems like that's what they were trying to do."

George opened the door and got out to look at the black oil on the windshield. "One thing's for sure—this isn't the kind of stuff you'd just happen to be carrying while you're driving around. They were definitely trying to kill us!"

Just after they cleaned the windshield and were climbing back in, the car phone rang. Nancy picked it up to hear Mr. Talbot, his voice tense and strained.

"Mrs. Malone, the clerk who checks the money into the vault, has just been taken to the police station for questioning," he said. "Apparently the insurance company's convinced that there's been some kind of monkey business about last week's cash receipts." His voice broke. "I can't believe she's got anything to do with what's happened. She's one of my oldest and most trusted employees. And the D.A. has just told me that a grand jury may be convened. If that happens, Nancy—if this ugly business gets into the newspapers—I stand to lose everything!"

"Don't worry," Nancy told him, trying to sound reassuring. "I'm sure we'll get to the bottom of this soon."

"I hope so," Mr. Talbot said. "It's not just the reputation of the hotel any longer—it's my whole future and the futures of all my employees that're at stake!"

Sheik Hassan Karim Abdullah's mansion was palatial and overlooked the ocean. The front courtyard, cooled by tall palms and filled with blooming flowers, had a waterfall that bubbled down over rocks into a pool. It looked like something out of a movie.

"The set's beautiful," George whispered as the three girls followed the sheik's male secretary through the courtyard. "But I can't say much for the cast." Two mustached and fierce-looking men had stopped them at the gate, and two others stood guard at the door to the house.

The secretary overheard George and smiled at her. "Of course," he said in a clipped British accent, "we must be very careful, for security. Sheik Abdullah has a priceless art collection." He opened the door and ushered them in.

Nancy swallowed. The hallway was like a museum, with huge oil paintings flanking both walls. Massive sculptures stood in each corner. A case at the middle of the hall held the most beautiful jewelry Nancy had ever seen. On the top shelf was a golden diadem studded with pearls and diamonds.

"Isn't that a lovely piece?" the secretary asked, following her look. "It's the crown Josephine wore when she was made empress. Sheik

Abdullah has given it to his fiancée to wear at their wedding this Saturday."

Nancy gasped. "Josephine's crown?" It had to be the very one that the empress wore with the Flame! Was this the connection they were looking for?

The secretary smiled. "You are quite right to be impressed. It is indeed a royal treasure. But come this way—the sheik is waiting."

"I don't believe this, Nancy," Bess said in a small voice as they continued down the hall.

Ahead, ten-foot-high double doors opened to reveal a spacious pillared room with a gold carpet running the length of its floor. On the far side of the room, behind a carved wooden writing table, sat a dark-haired man of middle height wearing a beautifully tailored business suit. He couldn't have been more than thirty, Nancy thought, but he looked like a king.

"His excellency, Sheik Hassan Karim Abdullah," the secretary said, bowing low. "I present to you Miss Nancy Drew and her friends, Bess Marvin and George Fayne."

Nancy stared. The gold carpet stretched for miles, and she couldn't bring herself to begin the long walk toward the sheik. Behind her, George gave her a nudge. "Go on, Nancy!" she whispered.

"It's all right, Miss Drew," the sheik said in a kindly voice as Nancy hesitated. He stepped out from behind his desk. "I'm afraid all this formality *is* a bit intimidating, isn't it?"

Nancy smiled, trying not to show her nervousness. "It's just that you don't meet real sheiks every day," she said.

"Then let's not be so formal," Sheik Abdullah replied. He motioned toward a corner of the room carpeted with Persian rugs and filled with pillows. "Come, we'll sit here and have some tea." He looked at Bess and George. "Or perhaps a soda?"

"A soda would be nice," Bess said, suddenly finding her voice.

"I understand that you're here to ask me about the Napoleon miniature," Abdullah said after a servant had brought them their drinks. "The one that I unfortunately lost to Mr. Kincaid." He sighed. "I have learned a good lesson—never bet on an inside straight."

Nancy tried to keep from smiling. "I suppose you know that the miniature was destroyed."

The sheik nodded. "What a pity. It was a most unique piece of art. Why, the frame alone was worth—" He broke off abruptly. "But of course, you have come to ask me whether I could have been responsible for its destruction."

Nancy slowly nodded her head once. Obviously Sheik Abdullah didn't believe in beating around the bush.

The sheik bowed his head. "I must often ask

forgiveness," he said contritely, "for my many faults. I am impetuous and inclined to extravagance, and I have a great love of beautiful women." He looked straight at Nancy. "But I do not carry the sins of extortion and arson on my conscience. You will have to look elsewhere for your—"

"Oh, Hassan! *Darling* Hassan!" A woman's excited voice interrupted from the back of the room. "The gown's just arrived. It was so beautiful that I couldn't resist trying it on—and the crown, too. Please, won't you take a moment to look?"

Sheik Abdullah beamed and stood up. "Of course, my dear," he said indulgently, holding out his hand. "I'm sure my guests will be interested to see it, too. Come and model it for us."

As Nancy turned to look, she gasped in astonishment. A radiantly beautiful young woman was walking toward them. On her head was Josephine's diamond-and-pearl crown. And the dress she wore was the Empress's Flame!

Chapter

Ten

"Nancy!" Bess gasped barely audibly, her hands flying to her mouth. "It's the Flame! And the girl who's wearing it is Sheila Sessions—you know, the movie star!"

"But it *can't* be the Flame." George was whispering too. Her eyes were fixed on the gown. "The Flame is gone!"

Nancy turned to Sheik Abdullah. "That's a marvelous gown," she said as calmly as she could. "Where did you get it?"

"It is a wedding gown fit for an empress," Abdullah boasted. "Indeed, it was designed for an empress—Napoleon's Josephine. Sheila will wear both the dress and the crown when we are married on Saturday. Come closer, Sheila, my love, so the girls can see. Nancy Drew, this is my fiancée, Sheila Sessions. Perhaps you have seen her in films."

"But the gown," Nancy persisted, her mind racing. "Where did you get the gown?"

The sheik smiled. "I bought it from a dealer in Venice who specializes in Napoleonic items."

Nancy stiffened. "Peter Wellington?" she asked.

"Yes, indeed." Abdullah looked surprised. "You know him?" To Sheila he said, "Thank you, my dear, for showing us the gown."

Nancy nodded grimly. "I know him. Are you sure," she asked as the movie star left the room, "that the gown is authentic?"

"Of course," the sheik said, sitting down again. "Wellington guaranteed it, and his reputation as a dealer is beyond reproach. And I certainly *paid* for an authentic gown—over a quarter of a million dollars."

A quarter of a million dollars for what had to be a copy! But Nancy didn't tell the sheik what she was thinking. Instead she asked, "Did Mr. Wellington himself make the guarantee? I mean, did you talk with him personally?"

The sheik looked thoughtful. "Well, no," he said. "I didn't. I spoke with his secretary on the telephone. She's the one who called to tell me that the gown was available. I made all the arrangements with her, and the actual transaction was done by a courier service called Security Unlimited."

Nancy raised her eyebrows. Secretary? Peter Wellington's shop wasn't large enough for a secretary.

Sheik Abdullah was watching Nancy shrewdly. "Perhaps you have reason to believe," he said, "that the gown my fiancée is wearing is not the authentic Flame." Nancy started to speak, but he silenced her by holding up his index finger. "If that is true, I only ask you to keep this to yourself. As long as Sheila is content with her wedding gown, I am content. The question of authenticity does not concern me."

"Well then," Nancy said, standing up, "I think we'd better be on our way. We have work to do." A little nervously, she held out her hand. Was there a special way of saying goodbye to a sheik?

"Thank you for coming, Miss Drew." The sheik took her hand and bowed deeply over it. Then he bowed to George and Bess. "I wish all of you the greatest luck in your search."

"Thanks," Nancy said fervently. "I have a feeling we're going to *need* lots of luck."

"Do you really think that Peter Wellington had anything to do with stealing and selling the copy of the Flame?" George asked as Nancy parked the car in a beachfront parking lot in Venice an hour later.

"I don't know," Nancy said. "But it's our best lead at the moment. I only hope that Mr.

Wellington is here so we can ask him about it. I'd like to talk to his secretary, too—if there *is* such a person."

The sign that hung on Peter Wellington's door read, "Out to Lunch."

"Speaking of lunch," Bess said brightly, "we haven't had ours yet." She pointed across the street to the café where they'd been before. "How about having a sandwich over there? Maybe that guy with the surfboard will stop in again."

George laughed. "Food and guys," she said teasingly. "The top two on Bess's greatest hits list."

But Bess wasn't paying any attention. She was already halfway across the street. "I think I'll have a Reuben," she said over her shoulder, "with *lots* of cheese."

The café was crowded, and the only table left was partly under a balcony. Bess relaxed happily in her chair after they'd given the waitress their orders. "I just love to watch the people in a place like this," she said. "Look at those kids over there. They look as though they've just walked off the set of a surfing movie."

"And those guys," George said, gesturing toward a flamboyant group with hair dyed all colors of the rainbow. "They could star in a science-fiction special. What costumes!"

"That reminds me," Nancy recalled. "When I talked to Brent this morning, he asked me about choosing our costumes for the party Friday night. Have you thought of what you'd like to be?"

"Maybe I'll go as Princess Leia," George said as the waitress set their plates in front of them. "I really like the way she—"

"Look!" Bess interrupted, tugging on George's arm. "Isn't that Chad Bannister?"

Nancy looked up. What was Chad Bannister doing in Venice? Had he come back to talk to Wellington? And if he had, why?

"Chad?" George exclaimed, looking delighted. Before Nancy could stop her, she stood up and waved. "Chad! Hi— Over here! It's George!"

At a table twenty feet away, Chad looked up with a smile, and then the smile froze on his face.

He jumped up and began to run toward them. "Watch out, George!" he shouted. "Run!"

To Nancy, events suddenly seemed to happen in slow motion. George had started toward Chad, but not far enough.

From the balcony above her, an enormous clay pot filled with trailing ferns had started to fall—straight for her head!

Chapter

Eleven

INSTANTLY NANCY REACHED out and shoved George as hard as she could. George stumbled forward but was clear of the plant. The pot crashed against the side of their table, smashing glasses and scattering dirt and green ferns.

"George!" Chad exclaimed, helping her to her feet. "Are you all right?"

"Just barely," George said shakily. "If that pot had hit me, it would have killed me!" She turned her head into Chad's shoulder and buried her face in his shirt.

People started to come over and ask if everything was all right. The manager rushed out and apologized, telling the girls to order whatever they wanted—lunch was on the house.

"Did you see what happened?" Nancy asked Chad after they were alone again.

Chad's arm was still around George's shoulders. "Not really," he said. "Whoever was sitting at the table on the balcony above you must have knocked the pot down by mistake. I looked up just in time to see someone push against it, and—"

Nancy asked sharply, "Did you see who it was?"

Chad shook his head. "No. And whoever it was was gone instantly."

Nancy looked up at the balcony. Chad was right.

Nancy took the outside stairs up to the balcony. A waitress was just beginning to clear away the half-eaten meal left there.

"Did you see who was sitting here?" Nancy asked breathlessly.

"No. My shift just started. The waitress who had this table left a couple of minutes ago. She was pretty mad, though. Whoever *was* at this table left without paying."

"Do you think it was the same person who tried to kill us on the highway?" George asked as Nancy came back down the stairs.

"I'd bet on it," Nancy said. "They probably followed us here."

"Should we call the other waitress at home?" Bess asked.

"I doubt it would do any good. I'm sure the person was disguised."

Back at their table, Nancy turned to Chad. "It was lucky for George that you happened to be here," she said casually. "Do you have business in Venice?"

Chad grinned easily. "No. I just thought I'd come down and see the sights," he said. His grin widened as he looked down at George. "You know, I was thinking after we said good night last night that I'd like to show you my boat. How would you and your friends like to go sailing?"

George threw Nancy an oh-let's-please look, and Bess gasped. "Go sailing? That'd be great, wouldn't it, Nancy?"

Nancy nodded. If they went sailing with Chad, maybe she'd have a chance to get something important out of him about his connection to this case. Besides, she'd thought of a couple more questions to ask Nicole Ronsarde, whose boat was at the same marina.

"Good," Chad said comfortably. "Then it's settled. How about today in a couple of hours?" As the girls nodded, he squeezed George's hand, then bent to kiss her. "Now you owe me for *two* rescues," he said with a grin and left.

"Isn't he great?" George said, watching Chad walk away.

Nancy hated to say anything, but she had to. "George," she cautioned, "I hope you won't forget that we're working. Chad Bannister is involved in this case somehow. And we've got to find out just how he's involved."

"Oh, I'll remember," George promised hastily. "I mean, I really like Chad, but—" She broke off and pointed across the street. "Hey, it looks like Mr. Wellington's shop is finally open." She sounded relieved. Obviously she didn't want to talk about Chad.

Nancy stood up. "Okay," she said. "You guys coming with me?" And the three of them crossed over to Peter Wellington's shop.

Mr. Wellington was engrossed in repairing a lacquered music box when Nancy, Bess, and George came into the shop. He looked up in mild surprise.

"Oh, it's you," he said to Nancy, and he went back to his work.

"Sorry to bother you again," Nancy said, "but I'd like to ask you a few questions about the Empress's Flame." She was watching him closely, but he made no visible reaction. Nancy went on. "I understand that your secretary made arrangements to—"

Peter Wellington cackled. "My secretary?" he asked. "Now, that's a good one. What would I want a secretary for?" He laughed again. "Except to dust things, maybe."

"I see," Nancy said. If that was true, then whoever had sold the gown could have been trying to throw suspicion onto Mr. Wellington.

That almost automatically took him off her list of suspects. Still, she had to be certain. "Well then," she asked, "do you know anything about the sale of the Flame to Sheik Abdullah?"

"To the sheik?" Peter Wellington looked up, surprised. "How'd Diana manage that?"

Nancy was listening carefully. It sounded as if he didn't know that the Flame had been destroyed. "I thought her uncle's will forbade her to sell any of his collection," he continued. "And anyway, what would Abdullah want with a dress? He collects jewelry and art—not costumes."

"He bought it for his fiancée," Bess said. "They're getting married on Saturday."

Mr. Wellington nodded. "I see, I see," he said. "So he bought the dress to go with the crown he bought last year." He sighed. "Of course, he can afford to buy what he wants. With all that oil money—" He stopped, frowning. "Do you hear something in the back room?"

Swiftly Nancy stepped to the green velvet curtain and pulled it aside. The small storage room was empty, but the back door was open. Somebody had been listening and left in a hurry.

She walked back to Mr. Wellington. "Nobody's there now," she said. "So, you're sure you don't know anything about the Flame? I'm sorry to keep asking."

Mr. Wellington shook his head. "Not a thing," he said.

Outside the shop, George stared at Nancy. "But you didn't tell him that you suspect that Abdullah bought a copy," she said.

"Well," Nancy replied, "he obviously didn't know that the Flame had been destroyed. That means—" She broke off abruptly. Down the street, hurrying off in the opposite direction, was Chad Bannister. Had he been the eavesdropper in Peter Wellington's back room?

"So we're going to Beverly Hills tomorrow to see Diana?" George asked. The girls were driving along the palm-lined drive to Marina del Rey to meet Chad.

Nancy nodded. "There are some things that keep bothering me," she said. "For instance, I want to know more about those burglar-proof display cases." She pulled the car over and stopped. "Well, here we are. We have a little time before we meet Chad, so I'd like to stop at Professor Ronsarde's houseboat, if you don't mind. I want to ask her a couple of questions."

Nancy led the way along the pier. She had changed into a blue-striped tank top and khaki shorts, and the afternoon sun was hot on her bare arms and legs. It was clear and breezy— perfect for sailing. But first Nancy had to ask

Professor Ronsarde whether she had ever met Peter Wellington. Maybe there was a connection between—

Nancy sensed something was wrong as they stepped up to the professor's houseboat. The front door was standing open, and a half-dozen cats were milling about on the deck, mewing plaintively.

"Oh, poor kitty," Bess said, bending over to pat one. "You look positively starved."

Nancy knocked at the open door, but there was no answer. All she could hear was the sound of a radio playing somewhere inside and the cats meowing around her.

"Look, Nancy," George said. She was pointing through the open door into the hall. "Do you think there was a fight here?"

Nancy stepped into the hallway and looked where George was pointing. The living room was a mess. Books that had been stacked were scattered around on the floor. The professor's green blouse lay crumpled in a corner. In the small galley kitchen a pan of cold eggs sat on the stove, and the faucet was running.

As Bess stepped into the kitchen and turned off the water, Nancy picked up the professor's blouse. What she saw made her heart leap into her throat. There, on the front, was a smear of blood!

Chapter

Twelve

Blood!" GEORGE GASPED, staring at the stained blouse. She looked up, her eyes round. "Do you suppose that the professor was—"

"Murdered?" Bess finished George's sentence for her.

"We can't jump to conclusions," Nancy said cautiously. "For all we know, the professor might just have gone out in a hurry. After all, she isn't exactly the world's tidiest person."

"But the blood?" George asked.

"There isn't much of it," Nancy said. "She might have cut herself or something."

Bess glanced pityingly at the cats. "Do you suppose we could at least feed the poor kitties? They're starving!"

"I doubt they're starving, but go ahead and feed them if you like," Nancy said.

While Bess fed the cats, Nancy and George checked with the people in the neighboring houseboats to see if anyone had noticed the professor leaving. No one had.

"What are we going to do, Nancy?" George asked when they were back at the professor's boat.

Nancy reached for the phone and began to dial 911. "Call the police, of course," she said.

Within minutes a uniformed officer was knocking at the door. He gave the houseboat a quick and thorough search, then turned to the girls. "There's not a lot I can do at this point," he said. "I'm going to file a report. If your friend doesn't show up within twenty-four hours, we'll investigate. Chances are Ms. Ronsarde will turn up safe and sound."

Nancy sighed. "Well, I guess that's the best we can hope for," she said. She turned to George and Bess. "We might as well go find Chad."

Nancy had hoped that the sail with Chad would yield some information about his background and his connection to the case, but it didn't. All she found out was what she already knew—that he was rich and cosmopolitan and that George was falling for him in a big way. He had a clever way of evading Nancy's questions while at the same time getting information out of George and Bess.

Nancy was glad that the girls didn't tell him anything important, like the fact that the sheik had acquired the copy of the Flame. But they did give him more details about the case than she would have liked.

Still, she couldn't blame them for not being able to resist his questions. Chad Bannister was one of the smoothest, most charming guys she'd met in a long time. And when she saw Chad wrap his arms around George and kiss her in the boat's little galley, she knew she might as well give up trying to get George to wring information out of him. George couldn't be objective anymore.

After the sail, Nancy and Bess said goodbye to Chad and drove home in the twilight. George stayed to have supper with him.

Nancy had already decided the next day on the way to Diana's that she needed to talk to Diana alone—without Amanda. Every other time they had talked, Amanda was there, speaking for Diana. Nancy knew she'd find out more if Diana didn't have Amanda to prompt her.

"Hi!" Diana said brightly, opening the door for the three friends.

Nancy did a double take. Diana was wearing a long dress with a full yellow skirt, red and blue sleeves, blue bodice, and a ruffled stand-up collar.

"Snow White, I presume?" Bess giggled.

"This is my costume for the gala at the Victory Hotel," Diana answered as they went into the elegant living room. "I've always loved the story of Snow White."

Nancy grinned. Now that she thought about it, Diana was a little like Snow White. It was just like her to wear such a childish costume.

"Anyway, what can I do for you?" Diana asked.

"I'd like to ask you a few questions, if you don't mind," Nancy said.

"More questions?" Diana collapsed onto the sofa. "I thought I'd answered enough questions. I mean, if you want information, you should ask that woman from the insurance company who was poking into everything this morning."

"You mean Elaine Ellsworth?" Nancy asked sharply. So, even though she had decided Preston Talbot was guilty, she was still investigating. Nancy wondered about this.

"Yes, that one," Diana said. She shuddered. "She's got the eyes of a fish."

"Diana, I need to know how the arsonist might have gotten access to the locked display case where the Flame was kept. Did anyone besides you have a key to the case?" she asked.

Diana bit her thumbnail thoughtfully. "A key

to the case?" she repeated. "Well, one of the servants could have copied my key, I suppose, but that seems—Amanda! It's nice to see you!"

Oh no! Nancy thought to herself. Amanda was standing in the doorway. "Hello, Nancy," she said. "Have you solved our crimes yet?"

A little frustrated, Nancy shook her head. With Amanda here, she knew that she might as well give up her questioning. Diana wouldn't talk for herself.

Amanda turned approvingly to Diana. "What a terrific costume," she said. "It's perfect!" She smiled at Bess and George. "Brent tells me that you're going to take your pick of the costumes at Kincaid Studios. You *are* coming to the party at the hotel on Friday night, aren't you?" Without giving them a chance to answer, she added, "I really hope you'll come. In fact, I want you to be my special guests."

"Thanks, but that's not necessary," Nancy said evenly. "Mr. Talbot has already invited us."

Amanda smiled broadly. "Well, it's settled then. You'll be there!" She settled herself on the sofa. "Please go on with your questions, Nancy. I didn't mean to interrupt."

But Nancy stood up. "I'm afraid we don't have time to stay," she said politely. "We need to get back." There was no point in hanging around any longer.

The girls said goodbye, went out to the car,

and headed back to the hotel, stopping for a bite of lunch. It was just past noon, and Nancy needed to bring Mr. Talbot up to date on their work so far.

In their suite, Bess was changing, and she looked ruefully at her red shoulders. "Looks like I got sunburned out on Chad's boat yesterday." She sighed.

Nancy frowned. "That was about *all* we got, I'm afraid. I didn't learn a thing from him about the case."

George stretched out on the sofa. "Speaking of learning things, why didn't you ask Diana any more questions? We didn't pick up any information there at all."

Nancy sat down in one of the plush chairs and put her feet up on the coffee table, the phone at her elbow. Mr. Talbot had been in a meeting, and she was waiting for him to return her call. "Well, I've got a hunch Diana's hiding something—something to do with the Flame. But we're not going to find out what it is when Amanda's around. Maybe Diana doesn't want Amanda to know what she's up to."

There was a knock at the door. "I'll get it," George said quickly, jumping off the sofa.

She opened the door, and three men in business suits pushed past her into the room. One of them was Sheik Abdullah's secretary. He marched toward Nancy. "You must come with us, Miss Drew," he said.

99

Nancy gestured toward the phone. "But I can't," she explained. "I'm waiting for an important phone—"

The secretary shook his head with a forbidding look. "You must come *now,*" he said sternly. He gestured to the other men. They stepped forward, and each put a firm hand on Nancy's arm. "You have no choice."

"Nancy, what's happening?" Bess whispered in a frightened voice.

"I'm not sure," Nancy said, fighting to stay calm. "It feels as though I'm being kidnapped."

"Indeed," the secretary said, arching his dark eyebrows. "You may call it whatever you wish. But you are coming with us—now." And the two men began to pull Nancy toward the door.

Chapter

Thirteen

GEORGE HAD BEEN watching, her mouth hanging open in disbelief. Now she leaped for the phone. "Whatever we call it, it looks like kidnapping to me," she said. "I'm calling the police!"

"That won't be necessary," the secretary said, grasping George's wrist. "I'm sure that Miss Drew will come with us willingly after she gives the matter some consideration. The sheik himself wishes to talk with her about a matter of great importance—the Empress's Flame!"

Nancy struggled away from the hands that restrained her. "I'll come," she said. "Just keep your hands off me!"

"But you can't go alone," Bess protested. "George and I are coming too."

"No," the secretary told her. "I have no instructions to bring others. Only Miss Drew."

"It's all right, Bess," Nancy reassured her as she picked up her purse. "Just stay by the phone so I can call you if I need you. And if I'm not back by night, call the police." She turned to the secretary. "Okay, let's go," she said. And, surrounded by her Arabian escort, Nancy marched out of the room.

The drive to Malibu in the sheik's enormous black limousine was silent. The secretary refused to answer any questions. But Nancy found out what she needed to know the minute the sheik greeted her.

"The Flame is gone," Sheik Abdullah said grimly.

Nancy stared at him. This case was beginning to seem like a game of mirrors—now you see it, now you don't. "Gone?" she repeated. "You mean it's been stolen?"

"No," the sheik said, clenching his fists angrily. "It's been confiscated. A woman from an insurance company—Elaine Ellsworth—came here with two policemen, claiming that the gown is material evidence in a case. I had to let her take it away." He frowned at Nancy. "I have told no one about purchasing the gown. *You* are the one who informed her. *You* are the one who must pay for this!"

Nancy shook her head. "I didn't tell her," she said. "Honestly, I didn't!" Her mind was racing.

How *had* Elaine found out about the sheik's purchase? Had she learned about it from Peter Wellington? As far as Nancy knew, he was the only other person who was aware that the sheik had the gown—apart from whoever had actually made the sale.

Perhaps Sheik Abdullah believed her. He waved his hand dismissively. "In any case, the matter of who informed the insurance company is not as important as making my fiancée happy. She is distraught over the loss of the Flame. You must do something."

"I know what to do," Nancy said.

She remembered that only a few days earlier Amanda had employed a costumer to make a copy of the Flame. "I think I could find a substitute. It wouldn't be the same dress you purchased, but it would look exactly like it."

This seemed to bring the sheik around to Nancy's side. "If you could do this," he said fervently, "I would be eternally grateful." He snapped his fingers, and the secretary appeared. "Please see that Miss Drew has all the money she needs to procure a substitute dress. And if you need any help," he said to Nancy, "you have only to ask."

"Thanks," Nancy said.

The first thing Nancy did when she got back to the hotel was call Amanda and get the name of the costumer. The phone was answered by her maid, who said that Amanda was out and would be gone for the whole evening. Nancy would have to try again the next day. She had just put the phone down when Mr. Talbot called.

"So the insurance company has the gown now," Mr. Talbot said after Nancy explained what had happened. There was a note of panic in his voice. "This thing is getting more and more complicated, and we don't seem to be any closer to a solution."

"I know," Nancy said. "I'm concerned too. But we have to follow each of these leads, Mr. Talbot. I can't tell when one of them might pay off."

"What about the Ronsarde woman?" Mr. Talbot asked apprehensively. "If something's happened to her, that puts a new slant on things. This extortionist may also be a kidnapper—or worse."

"I'm afraid you're right." And Nancy told him about the attempts on their lives. "I'm sorry I can't be more reassuring," Nancy added. "But I'm sure we've got to get a break soon. I'll let you know when we do."

After Nancy had said goodbye and put down the phone, George came into the room, her face glowing. She was carrying an enormous bouquet of red roses. "They're from Chad," she said in answer to Nancy's inquiring look. "And he sent a note asking me to go to the costume party with him."

Nancy sighed. George was obviously head over heels about Chad. "He certainly knows how to impress a girl, doesn't he?" she said.

George stiffened. "Don't you like Chad?" she asked, a little hurt.

Nancy gave George a searching look. "It's not that I don't like him. The problem is that Chad's definitely involved in this case—and we don't know how. Do you remember when we were at Peter Wellington's store yesterday afternoon and we heard a noise in the back room?"

Bess strolled into the room just then, obviously having been listening. "What are you getting at?" she asked.

"Well," Nancy said, "when we came out on the street again, I saw Chad running off in the other direction. Then Elaine Ellsworth shows up at Sheik Abdullah's and confiscates his fiancée's gown. The question is, who told her that the sheik had it?"

"Maybe it was Mr. Wellington," George suggested hopefully.

"Or maybe it was Chad," Nancy countered.

George frowned. "But why would Chad—?"

"Tomorrow I'm going to call Mr. Wellington and ask him if *he's* talked to Elaine," Nancy decided. She stood up and stretched. "In the meantime, I'm going to call Ned and crawl into bed for an early night. I'm bushed."

"Good idea," Bess said.

As she picked up the phone to dial Ned's number, Nancy turned to George. "Have you remembered anything else about the fire?" she asked.

George shook her head. "I keep trying," she said, "but nothing comes." She made a face. "I'm afraid it's hopeless."

Nancy's talk with Ned did a lot to raise her spirits. He missed her, he said. When she got back, maybe they could spend a long weekend at his parents' place at the lake. Just the thought of it cheered Nancy up. It had been only a few days since she'd said goodbye to Ned, but it felt like years. Talking to him wasn't as good as seeing him, but it was a lot better than nothing. Nancy fell asleep the minute she hung up the phone.

An hour later George gave a bone-chilling shriek from her bed. "Help me!" she screamed. "Help! I'm on fire!"

Chapter

Fourteen

Nancy jumped out of bed and rushed over to George. "There, there," she crooned. "It's only a bad dream, that's all."

George stared at her, wide-eyed, as Bess flicked on the light. "It was the brooch," she gasped. "It began to burn. It was the *brooch* that started the fire!"

"You're safe now, George," Bess said soothingly. "It was just a dream."

"But you don't understand!" George exclaimed. "The dream made me remember. The brooch on the gown—it suddenly got hot and began to burn."

"That's it!" Nancy exclaimed. "There must have been an incendiary device in the brooch itself." Then she frowned. "It's funny—I remember the brooch wasn't on the dress when we took it off you."

"Maybe it burned up," Bess suggested.

"Or fell off," George said.

"If it fell off," Nancy said excitedly, "it might still be lying on the bottom of the pool!" She snapped her fingers. "Tomorrow we're going to make a return visit to Diana's. But this time I think we'll make a very 'private' investigation."

"You mean," Bess said, "we're going to *sneak* in?"

Nancy grinned. "You've got it." She patted George's arm. "And now I vote that we all get some sleep."

Nancy was so tired that it was after ten on Thursday morning before she awoke. She immediately headed for the phone to call Amanda again.

"Hi, it's Nancy," she said when Amanda came to the phone. "I'm calling to get the name of the costumer at Kincaid Studios who copied the Empress's Flame for you."

"Sure. Let me just look it up in my book. What do you need it for?" asked Amanda.

Nancy hesitated. She hadn't promised the sheik to keep the wedding dress a secret. On the other hand, she still hadn't found out who had sold the stolen copy. And it probably wasn't a good idea to advertise the fact that the insurance company had possession of the gown now.

"Oh," Nancy said at last, "I just thought I'd like to ask her a few questions, that's all."

"Good idea— Wait, Nancy. The number's not here. I'd better check upstairs. Give me a few minutes, and I'll call back."

"Thanks," Nancy said and hung up. She was reading the room-service brunch menu when George came into the room rubbing her eyes sleepily. "How are you feeling this morning, George?" she asked.

"A whole lot better," George said. "It's great to be able to remember what happened, even if what I remember isn't all that pleasant." She looked at Nancy. "Did you reach Amanda?"

"Yes," Nancy said. "I'm waiting for her to—" She was interrupted by the telephone.

"Hello, Nancy? Bad news," said Amanda. "I've just called the studio, and the dressmaker's out of town for the next few days. I guess you'll just have to put off your questions. I gave them your number, though, and she'll call you back as soon as she can."

"But I can't wait a few days," Nancy said. "It's really important that I—"

"What can I say? I'm afraid you'll have to wait," Amanda said. "I'm really sorry." She paused. "Don't forget about Friday night!" she added brightly. Then she hung up the phone.

"What was that all about?" George asked.

Nancy sighed. "Just another snag in the case," she said. "I wonder if—"

Bess came in, pulling a pink top over her jeans. "Good morning, everybody," she said. "What's for brunch?" She reached for the menu. "What would you guys say to a crisp, hot croissant, with lots of butter?"

All during brunch, Nancy thought about her conversation with Amanda. It just seems too convenient! she said to herself. Why should the seamstress have gone out of town exactly when I need to speak to her?

Nancy decided to do her own checking. So when she finished eating, she picked up the phone and dialed Kincaid Studios. The operator at the switchboard transferred her call to the costume department, where she got a secretary.

"My name is Nancy Drew," Nancy said. "I'm an acquaintance of Brent Kincaid. I'm looking for someone who can copy a gown for me."

"Of course," the secretary said instantly. "I'll put you through to our chief seamstress."

After a minute's silence, a woman's voice said pleasantly, "Hello. This is Mrs. Terry."

"My name is Nancy Drew," Nancy said. "I'm looking for someone who can copy a gown in a hurry. It's a famous gown—the Empress's Flame. Maybe you've heard of it."

Mrs. Terry laughed. "Heard of it? That must be the most popular dress in Hollywood," she said. "I've already produced two copies."

Nancy's eyes widened. So this was the seamstress Amanda had said was out of town! And why had there been *two* copies of the dress? "Two copies?" she asked, trying to keep the excitement out of her voice. "Of course, you've already made one for Amanda Hyde-Porter. You made the other for—?" She paused, hoping Mrs. Terry would finish the sentence for her.

"That's the funny part," the seamstress said. "I don't really know who commissioned it. The whole thing was handled over the telephone, and I worked from a photo of the dress. A courier service picked it up."

"The courier service wouldn't have been Security Unlimited, would it?" Nancy asked. Sheik Abdullah had said they'd provided him with the Flame.

"Why, I think so," Mrs. Terry said in surprise. "How did you know?"

"Just a lucky guess," Nancy said grimly. "Anyway, I do need another copy of the Flame. Price is no object, but it has to be ready by Saturday. Can you do it?"

"Of course," Mrs. Terry said. "In fact, I still have plenty of the same material. I'll start on it right now. Things are slow today. Where do I deliver it when it's finished?"

Nancy gave her the sheik's address, thanked her, and hung up.

"Judging from the look on your face," Bess observed, "you've learned something important. What is it?"

"There were *two* copies of the Flame," Nancy told her.

"Two?" George asked. "You mean, one in addition to the one that Amanda had made up?"

Nancy nodded. "Mrs. Terry, the seamstress, said that the commission came over the telephone, and the transaction was handled by courier—Security Unlimited."

"So that's our next stop," George said.

Nancy nodded. "Come on," she said. "Let's go. I think we're really onto something this time!"

It was midafternoon by the time the girls finally made their way through the L.A. traffic to the offices of Security Unlimited.

"My name is Nancy Drew. I'm investigating an extortion case," Nancy told the woman behind the desk. "And I'd like to check your records. You handled two transactions recently. One involved the pickup of a package from the costume department at Kincaid Studios. The other involved the delivery of a package to Sheik Hassan Abdullah in Malibu."

The woman behind the desk stared at Nancy suspiciously. "Why should I tell you anything?" she snapped.

Nancy just smiled politely. "If I can't get these questions answered," she said, "the matter will be turned over to the police. Their investigators will take all your records down to the—"

With a sigh, the woman hauled out a large order book. "Let's see what we can find," she said, leafing through the pages. She stopped. "Here's the record of the pickup from the studio. The package was delivered here and picked up an hour later."

Nancy stared at the signature on the pickup line. It was indecipherable.

"What about the delivery to Sheik Abdullah?" George asked. "Maybe that will tell us something."

The woman turned several pages. "Here it is," she said. "A package was brought in to the office on Tuesday." She pointed to the book. "As you can see, it was delivered to the sheik's address an hour later."

"Do you happen to remember who brought the package in?" Nancy asked.

The woman shook her head. "The girl who usually works this desk quit yesterday. I don't know where she went."

Nancy wrote down her name and the phone number of the Victory Hotel. "If you should hear from her," she said, "here's where I can be reached." She thanked the woman, and the girls left.

Bess shook her head disgustedly as they went back to the car. "It looks as though we're really down a blind alley. We haven't found out a thing."

"Well," George said, "maybe something will turn up at Diana's."

Just then the car phone rang, and Nancy picked it up. "This is Nancy Drew," she said.

"Nancy Drew, this is Nicole Ronsarde," the heavily accented voice said on the other end of the line. There was a burst of static, and then Nancy made out the words "Calling from San Francisco."

"Professor Ronsarde!" Nancy exclaimed, pulling off the road and turning off the ignition. "We were just talking about you. We've been so worried. We stopped by to see you the day before yesterday. Your cats hadn't been fed, and the door was open. Are you all right?"

"Yes." The professor sighed. "I left in a hurry. I left a note for a neighbor, but it must have blown away. But she's taking care of my cats now. I am safe, so you don't have to worry."

"We found some blood on your blouse," Nancy said. "We were really worried about that."

The professor laughed a little. "Oh, I cut my hand slicing some bread. I didn't have time to clean up before I left." There was another burst of static. "Phoning about the manuscript," Nancy managed to hear.

"The manuscript?" Nancy asked. "You mean

Amanda's manuscript—the one that was burned?"

"Burned indeed!" Professor Ronsarde exclaimed heatedly. "The *Napoleon* is—"

Static nearly drowned out the rest of her sentence, and Nancy wasn't sure she'd heard it correctly. She sat staring at the phone in shock.

"What is it, Nancy?" George asked urgently. "What about the manuscript?"

Nancy shook her head, looking dazed. "If I heard right, Professor Ronsarde has discovered the manuscript that was supposedly burned. It's in the possession of a San Francisco dealer— and it's in perfect condition!"

Chapter

Fifteen

BUT I DON'T understand!" Bess exclaimed. "How could it be burned and still be in perfect condition?"

Professor Ronsarde was talking again now, and Nancy was listening. "A dealer called me yesterday morning to say that he'd bought the manuscript last week on the black market. He knew of my interest in the play, and he's letting me study it."

"But you're sure that it's the same manuscript?" Nancy asked. "It's not a copy?"

"But of course!" Professor Ronsarde said. "I am an expert in these matters. I *know* that this is the original."

Nancy thought fast. This new information eliminated Professor Ronsarde as a suspect—if she was telling the truth. But more than that, it opened up a whole new line of thought. Maybe the fire had been staged to cover a *theft*. "I've got an idea, Professor," she said. "But I need your help. Would you find a copier and send a copy of the first few pages of the manuscript to me at the Victory Hotel?"

"Yes, of course," the professor said. "I'll do it right away."

"Goodbye, Madame Ronsarde. Well," Nancy said after hanging up the phone, "it's beginning to look as if the manuscript that was burned was a copy. And *that* suggests that the portrait and the gown might have been copies, too—burned to cover the theft of the real thing!"

Bess looked totally confused. "I can't keep all this straight," she complained.

George sighed. "You're not the only one." She turned to Nancy. "But one thing seems clear. If Professor Ronsarde is the person who turned up the real manuscript, then she isn't the person who burned it, right?"

Nancy nodded. "I think we can take her off our list of suspects, and Sheik Abdullah as well. That leaves us with Peter Wellington. He wouldn't have destroyed the real things, but he might have stolen them and arranged for the burning of the copies. And there's another suspect." She glanced quickly at George.

"Oh no!" George said defensively.

"It could be Chad," Nancy said.

"Chad?" Bess exclaimed.

Nancy nodded. "We know that Chad was at the scene when the gown was burned. We know that he's talked with Mr. Wellington. It's entirely possible that he's masterminded this whole thing and that Mr. Wellington is in it with him. In fact, Peter Wellington might even be helping to dispose of the stolen originals."

George looked miserable. "It sounds so logical," she said. "But I just can't believe it. Chad's so fantastic!"

Nancy switched on the ignition. "Chad lives right behind Diana, doesn't he? Well, I suggest that we pay him a visit this evening to see what we can learn. When we're finished there, we can go over to Diana's and see if we can find the remains of that brooch." She looked at George. "Okay, George?"

"Okay," George said reluctantly. "But I'm telling you, I just don't believe that Chad's responsible for all this. I don't believe it!"

The expensive Beverly Hills neighborhood where Chad and Diana lived was quiet and calm in the early-evening dusk. Nancy parked a block from Chad's and they walked to the house. The Tudor mansion was large, imposing—and dark.

"I guess he's not home," George said. Nancy could hear the relief in her voice. "His car isn't even in the drive."

"That makes it easier," Nancy said. "Come on."

Checking to be sure they weren't being observed, Nancy led the others around to the back of the house. She tried the door of the garage. It opened easily. Stealthily Nancy went inside. The door from the garage into the kitchen was unlocked too.

"Are you sure we should be doing this?" George asked nervously, following Nancy into the kitchen. "What if Chad comes home and finds us?"

"I'll stay by the door and let you know if he drives up," Bess volunteered.

"Good," Nancy said. She went into the dining room. "I wonder why he doesn't have any furniture." She opened the door to a small room at the back of the house. "It looks as if he might be living in just this room."

Nancy and George stepped into the room and looked around. There was a narrow cot against one wall and a small desk and chair against another. On the desk were a microscope, a stack of books, and what looked like chemistry equipment.

George stepped over to the desk and picked up a manila folder full of papers.

"What is it?" Nancy asked.

George handed it to her. "I don't know," she said. "But it's got your name on it."

119

Nancy switched on a desk lamp. George was right. At the top, the file folder was labeled "Nancy Drew." It was full of newspaper clippings and notes about Nancy—her past cases, her father's name, and a description of his work as a criminal lawyer, even Ned's name and description. There were photos of Nancy, too, and a snapshot of Nancy, Bess, and George grinning into the camera.

"It's the picture Chad took yesterday while we were out sailing," George said, staring at it miserably.

Nancy put the folder down and picked up one of the books from the stack. It was a biography of Napoleon. Every book in the stack was about Napoleon. "It looks as though Chad's been doing some research," Nancy said. She glanced at the chemistry equipment. "And doing something else, too—something with arson, maybe?"

George picked up a piece of paper and turned it over in her fingers. Silently she handed it to Nancy. It was gray, with a distinctive red border.

"I guess we've found our extortionist," she said bleakly. "I'll wait for you outside." And without another word, she walked out of the room.

It was almost completely dark when the girls

climbed over the fence at the back of Chad's yard and crossed over into Diana's garden. Suddenly Nancy stopped. Just in front of them was a large floodlight. Unlike the other lights in the garden, it wasn't on.

"That light is probably part of an alarm system triggered by an electronic sensor," Nancy murmured. "We need to stay clear of it while we search."

"Where do we start?" Bess whispered. She glanced nervously over her shoulder at the sensor. "It's spooky in these shadows."

"How about the pool?" Nancy suggested. "It might have been cleaned, but it's still worth a try."

But they drew a blank at the pool. The bottom, shimmering in the soft underwater lights, was free of anything that looked like a brooch. Either the brooch had never been there, or it had been taken out when the pool was cleaned.

"Now what?" George whispered.

"Let's try under the balcony where you fell," Nancy said. "The brooch might have fallen off the gown when you went over." She began to search for it. Bess and George joined her, and after a minute Bess held something up to the light.

"What's this?" she asked eagerly.

George chuckled. "It looks like a bottle

121

cap. Nancy, I don't think we're going to find any—"

But at that moment Nancy's fingers touched something hard and lumpy. It was a small, blackened disk, half melted. The pin at the back was bent, and in the center, where the stone should have been, was what looked like a big glob of melted plastic.

"Here it is!" she exclaimed. "I've found it!"

Bess bent over to look. "Can you tell how it worked?"

Nancy pointed to the melted glob. "This was probably a plastic capsule of some kind, colored to look like a precious stone. It could have been filled with an acid, separated from another chemical by a barrier. When the acid ate through the barrier, it set off a violent reaction with the other chemical."

"And that's what made the gown ignite!" George exclaimed. "If you ask me, I'm lucky to be alive!" She bit her lip. "Do you really think that Chad—"

Swiftly Nancy put her hand over George's mouth. "Shh!" she said, pulling George and Bess deeper into the shadows against the house. "Somebody's standing above us on the balcony!"

There were footsteps on the balcony overhead, and then the sound of a frightened, tentative voice. "Who's out there?" Diana asked, her voice quavering.

And then, from the other side of the pool, a figure stepped out of the shadows—holding a gun. "Come out," he commanded brusquely. "Or I'll shoot!"

It was Chad.

Chapter

Sixteen

"STAY CLOSE TO the house," Nancy hissed, keeping an eye on Chad. "The pool lights are shining right in his eyes. If we're quick, he won't be able to see us." She grabbed George's hand. "Come on!"

As silently as they could, the girls crept single-file around the corner of the house. They scrambled over a small fence and then dashed behind the palm trees and down Diana's long drive.

Behind them, they could still hear Diana calling into the darkness and, after a minute, Chad's answering voice. But no one followed them.

"Whew!" Bess gasped when they finally reached their car. She collapsed into the back seat. "That was about as close as I want to come to being a moving target for a guy with a gun!"

George looked at Nancy. "So it is Chad," she said despairingly. There were tears in her eyes.

Nancy threw her a sympathetic glance. "We can't be sure," she said as she started the car and drove off. "But the evidence does point that way. Especially with the things we found in Chad's house. He could have rented the house as a front, so that he'd be close to the scene of the crime." Something was nagging at her— something didn't make sense. If Chad was policing Diana's house, how could he be a crook? But the rest of his actions seemed too suspicious to be ignored.

"What do you think he was doing at Diana's?" Bess wanted to know.

"I don't know. Maybe he pulled into his drive just as we were climbing the fence, and followed us over there."

"Do you think he recognized us?" George asked in a dull voice.

"My guess is that he didn't," Nancy said. "If he had, he would have called our names."

She fell silent, thinking rapidly. Now she needed a way to confront Chad—a way that would surprise him into revealing what he knew. And the germ of a plan was beginning to form in her mind. She turned to George. "Chad's going to the costume ball tomorrow night, isn't he?"

George nodded and shifted uncomfortably in her seat. "We were planning to go together," she said sadly. "I guess I'll break the date."

"I don't think you should, George. For one thing, we don't know for sure that Chad is our guy. For another, we need to be able to keep tabs on him. I think it's time we arranged a little surprise for him."

"You know, I'd almost forgotten about the costume party," Bess said. She turned on the interior light, leaned over the back of the seat, and put her hand on George's shoulder. "What would you think, George, if I went as Marilyn Monroe?" she asked, lowering her eyelids and pouting in an imitation of the blonde.

Nancy burst into laughter, and she was glad to see that George laughed a little too. They could always trust Bess to break the tension.

For a long time that night, Nancy lay awake thinking about her scheme. It was complicated, but it might just work. If Chad were the extortionist, he'd be bound to give himself away. At nine the next morning, she put her plan into action by calling Sheik Abdullah.

"Oh, Nancy!" the sheik exclaimed when she identified herself. "I am glad you called. The seamstress just brought the gown, and Sheila is ecstatic! It is magnificent. Nobody will know that it isn't the real thing."

He lowered his voice to a conspiratorial whisper. "In fact, I fibbed to Sheila. I told her that the insurance company had returned the original. So now she will never know that her dress is a copy." He chuckled over his little deception. "I hope that you and your friends will be guests at our wedding. And if there is any way I can show my gratitude, please let me know. I will be delighted to do it."

"Well, as a matter of fact," she said, "there *is* something I need to ask you. Would you mind if I . . ." And she told him what she had in mind.

There was a long silence. Then Sheik Abdullah sighed. "What you are asking is very difficult," he said. "Are you sure there is no other way to achieve your purpose?"

"I wish there were," Nancy said sincerely. "But I'm afraid there isn't."

"Very well, then," the sheik answered reluctantly. "I will do as you ask. You may expect your package before three this afternoon."

"Thank you," Nancy said. "Thank you very much." She hung up.

"What time are we going to the studio?" Bess asked, coming into the room. "I can't wait to pick out my costume." She grinned. "I've made up my mind—I *am* going to be Marilyn Monroe."

Nancy looked at her watch. "Well then," she suggested, "why don't we go now? I want to be back here before the middle of the afternoon."

But the phone rang just as they were getting

ready to leave. Nancy answered it. It was Amanda.

"I just wanted to be sure that you and your friends are coming to the party tonight," she said in a friendly voice. "It'll be a lot of fun."

"We're planning on coming," Nancy said. "In fact, we're on our way over to Kincaid Studios right now to pick out our costumes."

"Wonderful!" Amanda exclaimed. "Well, then, see you tonight."

Nancy frowned as she said goodbye and put down the phone. "Who was it?" George asked.

"It was Amanda," Nancy said. "She was making sure that we're going tonight."

"Well, we are," Bess said, picking up her purse. "Come on, let's go."

On the way over to the studio, Nancy told the others about her plan, and they talked over what they were going to do at the party. George had decided to go as Princess Leia. When they got to the studio's costume department, she went in search of a brown Princess Leia wig and a white dress. Bess raided the costume rack for a low-cut, lipstick-red dress with a tight skirt. She also found a pair of fifties-style spike heels to match the dress. Nancy found just what she was looking for—a floor-length fake ermine cape and a gold-colored crown studded with pearls. Then they all headed back for the hotel.

The three girls returned to the hotel with their

costumes at one-thirty. By three o'clock, Sheik Abdullah's promised package had arrived—a huge, fat box. Nancy opened it to make sure that what she needed was there, then closed it again and put it under her bed for safekeeping. She left Bess and George excitedly trying on their costumes and went off to tell Mr. Talbot what she had in mind.

When Mr. Talbot heard Nancy's conclusions about Chad and her scheme for the evening, he nodded. But there was a look of desperation in his eyes.

"I hope you're onto something, Nancy," he said. "Time's running out." He frowned. "This Bannister—if he's our man—could be dangerous. Use the hotel security police if you need them. And be careful."

"Wow!" exclaimed Bess as the three girls got off the elevator on the mezzanine, where the ball was being held. "What a great room!"

Nancy pulled her cloak tighter around her and looked around. The four-story atrium above them was filled with balloons, and in one corner a band was playing. There were palms and potted plants everywhere, and the area was already crowded with hundreds of costumed partygoers.

"Chad said he'd meet me at the fountain downstairs—in ten minutes," George said, consulting her watch. She patted her Princess

Leia wig nervously and looked at Bess. "Are you coming with me?"

"Do we have to go already?" Bess objected. She straightened her red skirt. "We just got here. I'd like to check the party out."

Nancy shook her head. "Business before pleasure, remember? And we agreed that George may need some backup. You two get Chad, and as soon as I locate Brent, Amanda, and Diana, we'll all meet in Mr. Talbot's office. With a little luck we'll be through in an hour or two and still have some time to party."

Nancy watched as Bess followed George down the stairs toward the fountain in the middle of the lobby below. Seconds later, she saw Brent walking toward her. He was dressed like the villain in a TV western—black hat, black shirt, black pants, black cowboy boots, even a black leather holster with an authentic-looking pearl-handled revolver.

"Oh, there you are, Nancy," Brent called as he made his way to her through the crowd. "I've been looking all over for you." He glanced around. "Where are your friends?"

"They've gone to meet someone who has some important information about the case," Nancy explained. "I've asked them to meet me in Mr. Talbot's office in a few minutes. Would you help me find Amanda and Diana? I don't want to be too businesslike at a party, but I think we're close to wrapping this up, and it would be a good idea if all of you were in on the conclusion." As she talked, Nancy kept glancing at Brent's gun. "You know, that thing looks real," she finally said.

"What? Oh, the gun." Brent laughed. "It's supposed to look real—real enough to fool the audience, anyway. But of course it only shoots blanks. What are you supposed to be, by the way? Wouldn't you be more comfortable if you left your cloak with the hat-check clerk?"

Nancy shook her head. "Thanks," she said, smiling slightly. "It's part of the costume."

Brent shrugged. "Whatever you say. Let's look for them over here—I think I saw Amanda."

Nancy and Brent had only walked ten or twelve steps before they were accosted by an older woman in a hideous chicken costume.

"Oh, hello, Brent!" she said excitedly. "I'm so glad I ran into you. I just heard about your portrait. What a terrible—"

"Hello, Grace," Brent interrupted her in a resigned voice. It was obvious that he wasn't crazy about talking to her right then, but he felt obligated to be polite. "Grace, this is my friend Nancy Drew. Nancy, this is Grace Murchison, an old friend of my father's. Yes," he added to Grace, "losing the portrait was a disappointment. But these things happen. It's really not all that important. Now, if you'll excuse us—"

"No, I suppose it isn't important," Grace

chirped. "At least, not for you. Your situation isn't at *all* like Amanda's or Diana's. I mean, losing those antiques must *really* have been a blow to them, what with *their* finances."

Somewhere in the back of Nancy's mind an alarm bell rang. "Their finances?" she asked out loud, not meaning to.

Grace fluttered the wings of her costume, obviously pleased to have an attentive audience for her gossip. "My dear, it's the very latest. I just heard it tonight. It seems that Amanda is going to have to start selling everything she owns to pay for those horrible investments she made on the stock market last year. As for Diana"—she clucked—"she's never been one to hang onto money. Her parties are fabulous, but her caterer told me just this afternoon that she still owes him money for the last—"

"We'll see you later, Grace," Brent said. He took Nancy's elbow firmly.

"Wait," Nancy objected. "I want to ask—"

"Hey, Brent!" The young man standing in front of them was dressed like a punk rock star, with a bright red double guitar slung over his shoulder. "I just wanted to tell you how terrific that demolition scene was in *Street Savvy*. You've got a real knack for special effects, man."

"Sam Brown—Nancy Drew," Brent said curtly. "Sam's my best stunt man, Nancy." He began to pull Nancy away, but she hung back.

"A knack for special effects?" she asked. Hadn't Brent told her that explosions weren't his line of work? That the studio had hired the best demolitions expert that money could buy?

Sam grinned at Nancy. "When it comes to pyrotechnics and demolition," he said, "Brent's got the touch. He's the best demolitions man in the business. Why, he builds whole films around fires and explosions."

Nancy stared at Brent.

Roughly, he grabbed Nancy's hand. "Come on, Nancy!" he commanded. "See you later, Sam," he added over his shoulder as he propelled Nancy through a door. Nancy stepped into an empty hall, hardly aware of where she was. Her mind was racing, putting everything together.

Amanda and Diana desperately needed money. Brent knew how to handle fires and explosives, and he probably had access to state-of-the-art materials that burned without a trace. There it was—means, opportunity, motive—and suddenly a half-dozen other ideas began to click.

Nancy whirled around to face Brent. "You!" she exclaimed. "It's been you three all along!"

Brent shrugged. "Why, of course," he returned affably. "But what are you going to do about it?" he asked slowly, raising his arm.

Nancy looked at his hand. She was staring down the barrel of Brent's drawn revolver.

133

Chapter

Seventeen

"THAT GUN *IS* real," Nancy said breathily. The four large bullets in the revolver's exposed cylinder obviously weren't blanks.

Brent smirked. "Right the first time. Now let's go for a ride." He gestured toward a service elevator. "Your friends are waiting."

"I should have known," Nancy said furiously. "It was so obvious!"

The door opened. Brent nudged her onto the elevator and pushed the Down button. "Well, don't be too hard on yourself," he said. "This plot's more complicated than any movie I ever put together."

After a few seconds the elevator door opened onto a loading dock at the rear of the hotel. In the dim light, Nancy could see George, Bess, and Chad—their hands raised—standing against a cement wall. In front of them stood Diana, wearing her Snow White costume, and Amanda, who was dressed as Catwoman in a black body suit. In Amanda's gloved hand was a small pistol, and she had a coil of rope over one shoulder.

"Well, well," Amanda said sarcastically when she saw Nancy. "If it isn't our wonder-girl detective."

Brent grinned. "Yeah, we're all here now. One big, happy family." He frowned slightly. "She seems to have the basic plot figured out, but I'd like to find out exactly what she knows."

"That might take a while," Nancy said. "Do you mind if I get comfortable?" She slipped the ermine cloak from her shoulders and let it fall to the ground. Then she took something out from under her arm and handed it to Amanda. "I believe this will prove what really happened to *Napoleon and Josephine*. It's a few pages from the manuscript you sold to a dealer in San Francisco."

Diana stared at Nancy, her mouth gaping open. "She's wearing the real Flame!" she blurted out, unable to believe what she was seeing. "She must know that the copy was burned!"

"Shut up, Diana!" Amanda snarled.

But Diana kept on talking. "You said that when we sold the fake gown to the sheik it'd be safe!" She dropped her head into her hands and began to sob. "Why did I let you talk me into this?"

"*I* talked *you* into it?" Amanda sputtered. She turned on Diana as if she'd forgotten that the others were there. "When you told me how much Peter Wellington wanted to give you for the gown, you practically begged me to arrange a scam for you. Since the terms of your uncle's will kept you from selling the dress, you had to be able to get the money out of it somehow."

"So you made a secret copy, in addition to the one we all knew about," Nancy said. "And *that's* what went up in smoke—not the real one. Just a worthless reproduction."

"Hardly worthless," Brent said in an offended tone. "Do you have any idea what a good reproduction costs these days?"

"But in the case of Amanda's manuscript," Nancy reminded him, "it didn't cost a cent. All you did was put a stack of papers into an envelope—an envelope that also contained one of your little high-tech fire-starting gimmicks." She glanced at Brent. "It was the same sort of gimmick that you dropped into my tote bag at the airport, I suppose. An incendiary device that works without leaving a trace."

Brent grinned. "Really neat, huh? It's a simple device—nitrated plastic that burns itself completely—but something that nobody's thought of before. It really had the cops and the insurance investigators scratching their heads."

"And you attached another of your little fire-starters to the copy of the Flame, didn't you?" Nancy continued.

George shook her head. "Whoa, back up! Let me get all this straight. The Flame that we were guarding was a copy? The dress that burned wasn't the original?"

"That's right, George," Nancy said. "All told, our friends here had three Flames. There was the original, which they hid. Then there was the copy Amanda and Diana made before we arrived, and which they planned to burn."

"Wait!" Diana cried. "It wasn't me! I didn't know anything about that first copy. Amanda and Brent *stole* the original and left me that fake. Then they told me I could only have part of the money if I cooperated with them. Otherwise, I wouldn't get the Flame back. They forced me to go along with their scheme!"

"But it sounds as though you were willing enough to make some money," George said to Diana.

Nancy nodded. "And then I suggested that a decoy copy be made—the third Flame."

Bess frowned. "So then, after the fire, they hid both the burnt dress and the decoy so that we wouldn't guess what had happened. And then they sold the unburnt copy of the Flame to the sheik." She paused, looking at Amanda. "Didn't you worry that the sheik would figure out that he'd bought a fake?"

"So what if the sheik *did* recognize the dress as a copy?" Amanda sneered. "We were safe, because he thought the dress came from Peter Wellington. He didn't know who he'd bought it from." She smiled mirthlessly. "Anyway, we still have the original. It's hidden at my house— and it ought to bring a fortune."

Nancy glanced at Brent. "You must still be looking for a buyer for your original miniature."

Brent laughed. "Well, actually, I'm so fond of it I think I'll keep it. I don't need the money." He gestured at Amanda. "I only got into this to help Catwoman dig her way out of a bad financial situation. And besides, it gave me a chance to pursue my favorite hobby—burning things up."

Nancy turned to Diana. "And you went along with their schemes because you couldn't sell the Flame. Your uncle's will prohibited it. So they promised to help you for a share of the profits.

"What threw me off," said Nancy, "was that it didn't occur to me that we were dealing with *three* criminals." She focused on Amanda. "I suppose it was you who posed as Peter Wellington's secretary, wasn't it?"

Amanda nodded, smiling slightly. "Good ploy, huh? And that crazy old professor—she was a terrific target for a frame-up."

"But by the time we got to the sheik," Nancy continued, "you must have been really desperate. Was it you and Diana who tried to wipe us out on the highway? And later, when we were having lunch in Venice?"

"I didn't want to do it," Diana whimpered. "Amanda made me."

George didn't see Amanda's grimace of disgust. She was looking at Chad. "But what about Chad?" she asked Nancy. "If they're crooks, how's he involved?"

"Yeah," Brent demanded. "Who are you—a cop?"

Chad didn't answer. Brent shrugged. "Well, it doesn't matter, anyway. You're in it now. Enough talking. Amanda, tie them up."

Amanda slipped the rope off her shoulder and began to tie Nancy's hands behind her back. "Looks like you came prepared," Nancy observed. "You've obviously been planning this for a while."

Amanda laughed. "Did you think we wanted you to come to the party just to have fun?"

Brent stepped over to a large open Dumpster at the edge of the loading dock. Halfway up one side was a latched door through which the trash was dumped. Brent swung the door open and kicked an empty soft-drink case in front of it.

"Don't tie their legs," Brent told Amanda as she finished tying Nancy's hands and began to work on George. "They need to climb in."

Diana's eyes widened, and her hand flew to her mouth. "What are you going to do with them?" she asked fearfully.

"What do you think?" Brent snapped, motioning to Nancy. "Get over here."

With Brent's gun at her back, Nancy climbed into the Dumpster. She was followed by George, Bess, and Chad.

At least we won't be sitting in garbage, Nancy thought. The Dumpster was empty except for several rolls of old carpeting and a couple of broken bottles.

"If you're lucky," Brent said, "this will be over in a hurry." Then he slammed the door behind them.

Through the metal walls they could hear Amanda talking to Brent. "Diana and I are heading back to the party to set up an alibi," she said.

"I'll be right with you," Brent answered.

There was a scratching noise—a match being lit?—followed by a soft hiss. A small metal canister with a smoking fuse sailed over the top of the Dumpster and landed on the roll of carpet.

Seconds later the carpet was ignited.

"Nancy!" Bess cried. "What are we going to do?"

"Well, we can't scream for help. That might bring them back," Nancy said tensely. The fuse was burning down fast. It looked as though they had about half a minute to free themselves. Nancy dropped to her knees and bent backward over the broken bottles. "I think we can cut ourselves free with these!" she cried.

Maneuvering across the floor, Nancy handed George a large piece of broken glass. In seconds George had cut Nancy's ropes. She scrambled for the canister, but as she reached for it a tongue of molten flame leaped out of a crack in the bomb. A choking, acrid stench filled the air.

"Nancy, get back! That's phosphorus!" yelled Chad. "It'll eat right through your hands if you touch it!"

Gasping, Nancy threw herself backward. The sizzling plume of flame arched down to the spot where she had been standing a moment earlier. Eye-burning smoke rolled as the acid hit the Dumpster floor.

Nancy grabbed another piece of broken glass and began sawing at George's bonds. By now the smoke was thick and choking, and the heat from the smoldering carpet filled the Dumpster. There was only a fraction of an inch left on the burning fuse!

Frantically Nancy sawed at the ropes on George's wrists. "I'm free," George yelled.

"Cut Bess loose," Nancy commanded, gasping for air. The long dress was hampering her movement horribly, but she managed to pull herself to the top of the Dumpster and drop down onto the loading dock.

With a wrench she swung the side door open.

"Come on!" she said. The other three were choking and gagging. "This thing's going to go any minute—we've got to get away!"

Bess and George yanked Chad out, his hands still tied, and all four of them dived around a corner of the building.

A split second later, the Dumpster exploded in a blaze of white-hot heat and flame, sending shards of shrapnel in all directions.

"Hey, when are you going to get around to untying me?" Chad asked, coughing.

"We'll untie you *after* you tell us who you are," Nancy said.

"I'm an insurance investigator," Chad said. "Elaine Ellsworth and I work together."

A broad smile spread across George's face. "Let's get him untied, Nancy!"

"Not so fast." Nancy laid a restraining hand on her friend's arm. "What about all that chemical equipment in your room?" she asked Chad. "And the file on me? And why did you rent that house, anyway?"

"I use the equipment to test for chemical residues in arson cases," Chad explained. "I had the file on you because I needed to know as much about you as possible. And my company rented the house for me because Elaine and I suspected that Diana's dress was the next target." He glanced over his shoulder. "Listen, we've got to be quick. Brent'll be back here any minute."

"Okay, George, untie him," Nancy said. She glanced at the Dumpster. Flames and smoke were billowing out the top; a fire alarm in the hotel had just gone off. "Come on, let's hide so we can get the drop on our would-be murderers."

She pointed to a pile of large cardboard boxes in the shadow of the loading dock. "Quick. In those." She and Bess climbed into one, and George and Chad got into another.

As the lids fell down, the loading dock became noisy with people. Five hotel employees rushed out with fire extinguishers, and two others were pulling a canvas fire hose through the door. Behind them, a half-dozen curious partygoers had gathered to watch. Far in the distance, sirens began to wail.

At one side stood Brent, Diana, and Amanda —directly in front of the cardboard boxes hiding Nancy and her friends. They had no idea they were being overheard.

"I still wish we hadn't done it," Diana said plaintively. "Extortion is one thing, but murder—"

"Relax, Diana," Brent replied. "You're safe. Nobody's going to find out what happened." He laughed a little, as if he were savoring the moment. "Just *look* at those glorious flames!"

Chapter

Eighteen

B RENT KINCAID," CHAD said, stepping out of his box. "You're under arrest."

Brent whirled around. "How did you—?" As he was reaching for his gun, Nancy grabbed his arm and twisted it behind him. The heavy weapon clattered to the pavement. Diana screamed and threw her arms around Amanda while Bess dived for the gun.

At that moment Mr. Talbot rushed through the loading-dock door, followed by three guards. Elaine was on his heels.

"Nancy! Thank heavens you're all right!" Mr. Talbot panted. He glanced from the burning Dumpster to Bess, who was training the revolver on Amanda, Diana, and Brent. "What's going on here?"

"These are our criminals," Nancy said.

"It wasn't me!" Diana babbled hysterically. "I didn't have anything to do with it! I was forced to go along with them!"

Brent threw Amanda a black look. "I *told* you we couldn't count on her," he growled. "But you had to pull off one more. If we'd stopped at two, we would've had it made!"

Elaine turned to the guards. "Take these three away and hold them," she said. "The police are on their way." She reached for Brent's gun. "And take this, too—as evidence."

"Thanks," Bess said. "That gun was getting heavy."

Chad grinned at Nancy. "I've got to hand it to you," he said. "You've untangled the most complicated insurance fraud I've ever investigated." He glanced at her dress. "But there's one thing I don't understand. Where did you get that dress? And why did you wear it tonight?"

Nancy glanced down at herself. The Empress's Flame—the copy she had borrowed from Sheik Abdullah—was a total mess.

Nancy gave a rueful sigh. "It belongs to the sheik," she explained as Elaine came up to listen. "Elaine confiscated the copy he'd bought from Amanda. But his fiancée, Sheila, had her heart set on wearing the Flame for her wedding tomorrow. So he had another copy made for the wedding." She grinned at Chad. "I wore it to try to surprise *you* into a confession."

"Me?" Chad looked astonished.

Pulling off her Princess Leia wig, George walked up beside Chad. "We thought you were the arsonist," she said with a giggle. "Especially after we found all that equipment in your room. And then you clinched it by pulling a gun on us while we were searching Diana's garden for the brooch."

"Oh," Chad said. "So that was you! I thought it was burglars."

"This case has been crazy," Bess said. "I feel as if we've been playing hide-and-seek all week." She sighed happily. "But all's well that ends well."

"But it's not going to end well for Sheik Abdullah and Sheila," Nancy reminded her. "There's no way Sheila can wear this dress tomorrow. It's a mess." She looked questioningly at Elaine Ellsworth. "Unless—you've got the sheik's copy. We could return it to him in time for the wedding." She paused and smiled. "Or maybe we could let him have the *original* Flame, the one Amanda has hidden at her house. After all, he helped out by lending me this dress."

Ms. Ellsworth frowned. "Well, it's a little irregular—"

"Oh, come on, Elaine," Chad said with a grin. "Be a sport. After all, it *is* a wedding. We can make the swap afterward, and the sheik can have the copy he bought."

"Oh, all right," Elaine Ellsworth said. "I'll ask the police to turn the gown over to us tonight."

Mr. Talbot was beaming. "So the case is completely wrapped up?" he asked.

Nancy, Elaine, and Chad nodded together.

"Terrific," Mr. Talbot said with an enormous sigh of relief. "How about coming back to the party now?"

Bess looked down at herself. Her Marilyn Monroe dress was torn in two places, the heel had broken off one of her shoes, and her blond hair was disheveled. "Come back to the party looking like this?" she asked in horror. She wrinkled her nose. "And I smell even worse."

"You could masquerade as one of the heroines in an arson mystery," Chad said, slipping his arm around George's shoulders. And they all laughed.

"That was a wonderful wedding!" Bess sighed. She and Nancy were sitting in the back seat of Chad's car on the way to the airport late Saturday afternoon. George was in the front seat with Chad.

"Didn't Sheila look terrific in the real Flame?" George asked. "She's so beautiful—just like an empress."

"Well, here we are," Chad said, pulling up in front of the airport. "Victory Airlines is right through that door." He got out of the car, opened the trunk, and began to help them with their luggage.

"Next time you come to L.A., Bess," George said, hoisting one of Bess's suitcases, "send your clothes air freight."

Chad grinned. "Next time you come to L.A.," he said, putting his hands on George's shoulders, "how about letting me know?"

Nancy nudged Bess. "Let's go check on our tickets," she suggested with a smile.

"Oh, but I want to say goodbye to Chad," Bess objected.

Nancy pulled her away. *"George* is saying goodbye to Chad," she said pointedly. "They don't need us."

Suddenly a man in a business suit stepped in front of them. "Miss Drew?" he asked in a low, gravelly voice. Behind him Nancy saw two other stern-faced men. They were blocking her way.

"Uh-oh," Bess said. She stepped behind Nancy. "I thought this case was all wrapped up. Don't tell me there's *more!"*

Nancy swallowed. "I'm Nancy Drew," she said.

The man relaxed and smiled. "Then I am glad that I caught you before you boarded the plane," he said. He reached into his pocket and pulled out a small package. "Sheik Abdullah wanted you to have this as a token of his respect and gratitude. He would have presented it to you himself at the wedding, but he was preoccupied with other matters. You understand, I'm sure."

Nancy nodded and smiled and began to open the package. Inside was a small white box.

"Be careful, Nancy," Bess cautioned. "Who knows what it might be."

Cautiously Nancy lifted the lid. Then she gasped.

"It's a ruby pendant!" Bess exclaimed. "Oh, how beautiful!"

Nancy held up the necklace. The ruby's light glinted fiery red.

"It's another glorious flame," she said. "The nicest one of all!"

Nancy's next case:

Wendy Harriman, the most popular cheerleader in Nancy's high school class, invites her old schoolmates to a beach party. But the reunion stirs up much more than memories. Someone deliberately sets a flash fire at the barbecue pit—then Wendy's room is ransacked and robbed.

When Nancy investigates, she discovers Wendy isn't as popular as she seems. A few fellow students still carry grudges against the snobbish teen queen. Nancy also finds that her former boyfriend Don Cameron is still carrying a torch for her, which makes Ned see red. But romance takes a back seat to the mysterious crimes that plague the party guests. Can Nancy figure out who among her old friends may be her worst enemy ever? Find out in *MOST LIKELY TO DIE*, Case #27 in The Nancy Drew Files℠.